CONTEMPORARY AMERICAN FICTION

A VISIT TO YAZOO

Charles Neider's distinguished career as novelist, Mark Twain scholar, and Antarctic traveler has spanned forty years. His fiction has been praised by Saul Bellow, Aldous Huxley, E. M. Forster, Thomas Mann, Marianne Moore, and other prominent authors. One of his novels, *The Authentic Death of Hendry Jones*, was made into the cult movie *One-Eyed Jacks*, starring Marlon Brando. Neider has written a novel and two nonfiction books about Antarctica, which are highly regarded by William S. Buckley Jr., Norman Cousins, and Alfred Kazin, among others.

A VISIT TO

CHARLES NEIDER

YAZOO

PENGUIN BOOKS

PENGUIN BOOKS
Published by the Penguin Group
Viking Penguin, a division of Penguin Books USA Inc.,
375 Hudson Street, New York, New York 10014, U.S.A.
Penguin Books Ltd, 27 Wrights Lane,
London W8 5TZ, England
Penguin Books Australia Ltd, Ringwood,
Victoria, Australia
Penguin Books Canada Ltd, 2801 John Street,
Markham, Ontario, Canada L3R 1B4
Penguin Books (N.Z.) Ltd, 182–190 Wairau Road,
Auckland 10, New Zealand

Penguin Books Ltd, Registered Offices:
Harmondsworth, Middlesex, England

First published in Penguin Books 1991

1 3 5 7 9 10 8 6 4 2

LIBRARY OF CONGRESS CATALOGING-IN-PUBLICATION DATA
Neider, Charles, 1915–
A visit to Yazoo/Charles Neider.
p. cm.
ISBN 0 14 013404 2
I. Title.
PS3564.E268V5 1991
813'.54—dc20   90-38158

Printed in the United States of America
Set in Linotron Janson
Designed by Kathryn Parise

TO MY FRIEND

JAMES COHEE

A VISIT TO
YAZOO

HAVING RETIRED, OR RATHER HAVING *BEEN*
retired, Burbank was on his way to some fishing off the Keys when a series of odd events came his way. There was with him at the time old Mama Duck (Ethel his wife), always tagging along on his sporting trips despite what the doctors had warned. There was also Flora the boxer, a tan, smoothcoated, swinish piece of flesh whom he called Gristlehead or Knucklehead. And there was Nuncle the parakeet, perched on the steering wheel and cocking one tough eye at the road heading south. Burbank, driving an Emperor, was somewhere on the Eastern Shore doing about ninety, which was practically crawling when you considered the special engine of his special, all-American car. Ethel was somnolent, as she always was on his motor trips, and Flora was asleep on the rear seat among bits

and ends of luggage and clothing, breaking wind now and then, so that he had to drop all the windows to the autumn air, which he did with a flick of his finger.

"Can't you do something about her?" he complained.

"What do you suggest?" Ethel retorted.

She was tired of his badgering her on the subject.

"Shoot her," he said, knowing that Gristlehead was her darling.

It was Thanksgiving Day but Burbank didn't feel he had much to be thankful for. He should have been at a football game, sitting as usual in the thinnest of topcoats (he was warm-blooded and still very vigorous) and with a flask, bathed in and by the Old Spirit, his consciousness beautifully dimming into a better world of manly sports and comradeship. But personal relations, as he had long known, especially when in his cups, had gone to the dogs in this country, so it was no wonder that he, an eminent American, an eminent all-American (no pro-Jap, pro-German, pro-Swede, pro-English he; it was a wonder he didn't have a major stroke when he contemplated all the foreign cars that had swamped and almost wrecked Detroit), was exposed to the barrenness of a Thanksgiving Day on the road. He was on the wagon again and there was this dryness in his bones that made him fear they were about to crack. A drought, a drought, a drought in his very soul! And all the northeast drought he had been reading about, the forest fires, the low reservoirs, the dust, the flying topsoil, only (and relentlessly) reminded him of the personal drought he was enduring.

And now came the moment when his engine, all chromed, all aglisten with the finest oil money could buy, let him down. Why did it do it? Because into the customizing process there had crept one fatal flaw, the result of which was this. A chip flew off the oversized crankshaft and got in the way of a connecting-rod bearing. The bearing jiggled the connecting rod. The rod screamed at the piston. And the piston shouted hysterically at the cylinder wall and beat its head madly at everything in reach. In addition, the scallop formed by the chip set up a vibration which at the engine's present throttle fanned Nuncle's tail, jerked Flora's ears, jounced Ethel's cheeks and caused Burbank's heart to miss several beats. There was a pounding as if an anvil was being hammered under the hood, until he imagined for a moment the black hood itself billowing under the shock waves. To have a thing like this happen to you on the road on Thanksgiving Day in the sticks was enough to make the stoutest heart panic, and Burbank if he had anything had a stout heart. It sounded like the knock of doom— but only for a millisecond, for Burbank, used to rude shocks as the diet of banking, braced himself quickly, made several internal adjustments and was ready almost instantly to deal with the outer world and to do it in his vigorous, headstrong, confident, almost savage fashion.

At this moment the metal, which after all was only metal and not flesh, could no longer bear the strain, so the engine, this chromed, beautifully glistening engine, this great all-American engine, gave up the ghost. His luck, however, had not run out, for by George if at the bottom of the hill, where the hill met an extensive plateau furred by trees, there wasn't a motel and across from it a garage. They were the only buildings in sight in this sweep of naked fields, far stands of cold trees and wet sky. He coasted into the motel driveway and bounced out of his leather bucket seat ready to deal with the situation whatever it might be. He had traveled widely, had mingled with the greats and near-greats of this world, had made his way up by his own efforts and talents and with the theory that trouble was as much a part of the game as success. Therefore he knew what to do when trouble came, as it had.

The first thing to do was to let people know exactly what you expected of them, and with the least expenditure of energy and time. So he said brusquely to his wife, "You register. Be sure and get a room away from the road," and prepared to cross the highway to join the two lean men lounging in the waning light against a wall of the ramshackle garage. He had an uneasy feeling they were standing there just to enjoy the failing light and weren't in a mood to work at the end of this Day of Thanksgiving.

"Okay," Mrs. Burbank said in her tremulous, musical voice.

Wearing a tan tweed suit and brown alligator shoes, she went to the office at once, her brown alligator bag under her arm.

Several cars going at great speed caused Burbank to pause on the highway shoulder. He gave the motel and the Emperor an appraising glance. You wouldn't have dreamed, looking at it as he did now, that the Emperor was sick. Why, it was as slick as a seal and just as black and trim. What looked sick was the motel, the kind you'd expect out in the middle of nowhere, with its yellow brick, probably jerrybuilt rooms, its tiny restaurant near the office, its no doubt brokendown beds and lukewarm water. He wouldn't invest a dime in a place like this. As for its name, staring down at him from a large sign, it couldn't have been stupider: THUNDERBIRD. And as if that wasn't enough, they had set up a huge sign to dominate the sky, a bird that was neither eagle nor sparrow nor good American turkey, just a spread-eagled *thing* with formalized wings and claws, its beak pointing south.

THUNDER-bird! He could still hear the thunder of the Emperor in his mind and then the infinite, somehow welcoming silence. "Ought to be a wooden Indian up there, not some bird that looks like no bird that ever lived or died," he thought. There was something unpleasant about it. It brooded against the darkening sky and resembled, even if faultily, a bird of prey. The sign burst into neon flames, the bird did the same, and damn if the eyes didn't blink as if they were emitting bolts of lightning!

The road being free now, he crossed it quickly, having stuck his fists into his slash pockets. Hatless, he wore a gray tweed jacket and charcoal flannels. He would speak at once to the men and let them know exactly what was on his mind. But before he could speak to them one of them said, "Was that *you* coming tearing like hell's busted loose down the hill?" Burbank was startled. It hadn't occurred to him the sound of his trouble had carried so well.

The man, standing with his hands behind him against the old, discolored wall, wearing beatup overalls, his shoes scuffed and greasy, standing in dirt, his hands blackened, his nails black and horny, seemed to take a personal interest in him— for obvious reasons: his hairy ears (black hair sprouted from the tops of them as well as from the insides) were attuned to car trouble. He no doubt considered him, Burbank, lucky to have conked out in such a spot. But he didn't seem impressed yet by him and Burbank didn't like this, nor the languid nasal drawl and the assumption of equality. (Black hair sprouted from the nostrils too.) The assumption of equality led him to suspect he was going to have trouble, more trouble than he already had.

"She's probably locked," the second man said.

"Meaning just what?" Burbank demanded.

These men weren't eager for business, and any American not eager for business made Burbank uneasy, Thanksgiving Day or not. If they weren't here for business just what were they here for? He could see he might have to look up the owner or the foreman, or somebody. He wouldn't mince words once he did. The second man didn't reply.

"He means," the first man began, then paused to smile, revealing teeth speckled by caries, meanwhile looking Burbank over pretty thoroughly.

"She's jammed up, your engine," he said, and despite his smile his eyes were icecold, with the veneer of enamel on them.

He was an ordinary-looking man, a common man of the fields, a cracker, and Burbank knew he wouldn't have the problem of remembering him, for the simple reason that there would be no impression to forget. This simple thought warmed him at a moment when a gust of warmth was welcome, for he had shivered slightly: the air was cold and the afternoon was waning fast. He thought a moment, regarding the men as they regarded him; then, remembering his Emperor's present unbelievable condition, said, "Anybody around here know how to fix my car? I need some help."

"You sure do," the second man said, but made no move to help him.

Their Southern drawl vaguely menaced him.

The second man was more unusual than the first although he was dressed exactly like the other, and Burbank couldn't help but admire him. The anatomy of the man's face showed through his skin: tendons, bones, high points, hollows. A John Carradine of the garage world. Burbank envied him his extreme leanness, not only because he admired leanness as he did tallness but because he had been told by someone that it was wise, as the French put it, to age dry. But he, Burbank, old mesomorph, was never going to attain the heights of leanness this cracker came by naturally. The cracker would have worn tailored clothes well. The irony of it was that he probably had only one good suit (his church and Grange one), and even that probably looked wooden on him. Meanwhile there was no sign of life from the garage and no least sign of life elsewhere. Life was at a standstill down here on this Day of Thanksgiving.

"Locked, you say?" Burbank inquired.

Instead of replying, they started across the highway toward the Emperor, and instead of leading he was forced to follow. These Eastern Shore men were tall (at least they were taller than he) and he had had to look up at their faces as he spoke to them, as he had had to look up at the faces of so many men in this world. Glancing at their backs, he recalled their hard eyes, dead hair, creased faces, teeth stained by tobacco juice. Locked? He had never heard the word used in this way. The man had meant fused, probably. Burbank had a vision of his engine fused and felt shame in his strong, short, calvy legs.

The men went up to the Emperor in a manner very democratic, as if to say, "We rough-and-tumble boys aren't impressed by dough and city slicks." But when they lifted the hood they whistled and exchanged glances and studied Burbank for a reappraisal, for they saw the tappet covers in their chromed glory, and all the other chrome, enough to dazzle any real American. He ought to have taken heart, but at this moment, the day fading fast, having almost merged with twilight, and it being a kind of American holy day, yet with no sign of turkey or pumpkin pie or cornucopia of native fruits and veggies to cheer him, he couldn't find it in him to do so.

The second man twisted the gold key in an effort to start the Emperor. Only a troubled stillness answered him.

The first man said, "She may *be* locked."

The second man said, "Hell. She *is* locked."

The first man said, "She may *be*. At *that*."

The second man said, "Shit. I *know* she's locked."

And Burbank stood there listening to this cracker music without at all appreciating it.

"So? What now?" he asked, and he couldn't help but wonder

if his lame tone wasn't due to his being prematurely retired.

The first man said, "We'll tow her to a garage in Yazoo. In the morning. We're not set up for this kind of job."

"Push her to my room. What's the number?" Burbank inquired of his wife, who had emerged from the office and was holding a key.

"Eight," Mrs. Burbank said mildly, blinking.

They pushed the Emperor with Burbank and Nuncle at the wheel. He slipped them a tenspot and was glad to see them go. Unable to leave the Emperor alone, feeling an American itch to do something about it (a wholesome itch in the old, simple auto days but nowadays often leading to high-tech despair), he released the hood catch, lifted the hood and lost himself in wonder and admiration beneath it. But the case was beyond him, as he well knew in advance. The surge of high technology had overwhelmed him, which he knew as well as any good American. He stared at the tappet covers in their chromed glory. When it came to *them* he wasn't in the mood to glare, for they carried his name, and if there was one thing he took seriously and *had* taken seriously it was himself—until he took to drinking too much at parties, or to staggering, or to belting somebody, or to passing out. He had had his name engraved proudly on the tappet covers after the customizing people had assured him it was the thing to do. Now he felt ashamed because he had done it, ashamed because of what had happened to the Emperor. CHRISTOPHER ANDREW BURBANK, done twice in Gothic letters. But it was still a name to conjure with, even if he *was* prematurely retired.

Mrs. Burbank, meanwhile, having let herself into the room, had stretched out on the bed nearest the door. They always ordered twins, not because either of them kicked but because Burbank had dreams that made him squirm and often waked him, then left him lying there, muscles aching or twitching, mind overpowered by images and thoughts. For example, there was this dream he had had last night: a quiet street, a small town, an arc light, a store window (a corner, near a tobacco shop, closed), and Marlon Brando lying naked in the window, one knee flexed, a woman massaging his scalp, and a passerby peering, saying, "Look at his fire hole!" Then Picasso coming out and painting, canvas flat against brick. The back of Picasso's head, neck. Picasso slashing paint on, wild. Suddenly peeking at it through two fingers, careful. Then scraping excess off (gooey, clayblue, cold) and dripping a cupful into Burbank's hand. And Burbank feeling the weight, the pride, and wanting to shout that Picasso had honored him, yet sensing what the goo meant, a heavy moist mass embarrassing him, which he would have to dispose of somewhere quietly, then work to wipe his hand. And the night before last he had dreamed he had bought an apartment: huge, but he had been nodding when he examined the contract, for the very first night he discovered another couple (the next-door neighbors) sharing the master bedroom. He had tried to sleep but had failed. It was uncanny to hear them shifting around in their sleep and to think that in this apartment, *owned* by him, there was no solace or privacy even in the master bedroom.

Poor Mrs. Burbank, she had to tolerate everything, even his recital of his dreams. She rested now with closed eyes, probably hoping to snatch a little solitude before he came on stage again. But he came on quickly and repeatedly, carrying their own suitcases (two for her); a briefcase; Nuncle's suitcase (just as real a Mark Cross as theirs, with NUNCLE engraved in gold under the handle); Flora's blanket and pillow, real bone and rubber bone, vitamins, currycomb, canned food, food bowl and water bowl; Nuncle himself, now in his gilded cage; and assorted items of clothing. Having deposited these things, he opened Nuncle's suitcase and set out the bird seed, the treat seed, the vitamin seed, the cuttlebone, the toys for inside the cage, others (like the ladder) for outside, the cage cover and—very important—the Princeton water, for Nuncle was susceptible to the travel trots.

By now, understandably, Burbank was in a pet. He was displeased with the Emperor, with Ethel and with Flora and was still unable to forgive the hayseed owner for having spoiled the sky with that spread-eagled no-account *bird* he had put up there. Seeing Ethel stretched out as though dead (she had covered her legs with the spread, was always cold, poor thing), he examined the room, poking his head into the musty closet with its film of reddish field dirt (Lord how the scent of the dirt made him want to wet his tonsils with a bourbon and soda), into the bathroom with its tiling which he was positive was imitation even without tapping it, just as he was certain the walls were board and not lath and plaster, and looking outside behind the magenta drapes at the driveway and autumn fields.

"Well, what's wrong with the Emperor?" Mrs. Burbank asked in a tremulous, musical voice.

"You wouldn't understand," he growled.

"How long will we be here?"

"I'm going to have me a bourbon before dinner."

"Papa *Duck!*" she cried, sitting up and controlling an impulse to feel panicky.

He wished he could clobber her. But first there was the fact he was a gentleman (the Institute years rose in a mellow cloud before him), and second that her heart might not stand up to it. It was a pitiful heart, had a way of throwing a fit whenever it felt like it. A wonder she was still alive and he still sane. She had suffered so much, poor old woman. God bless her, poor old thing.

And there was that Flora, that meat-head, lying on the floor beside her. Flora twisted her eyes at him like a rhino, refusing to move her head, which rested before her on the rug. He knew from that shifting of eyes, that immobility of skull, what she needed and gave it to her: a boot in the can, hard enough to make her wince, yet not so hard that Mama Duck could really have something on him.

"*Thunder*-bird," he said acidly, jamming his meaty hands into his deep slash pockets.

"Be thankful we're off the road."

"*Thunder*-bird."

"Better than out on the highway."

"THUNDER-bird."

"Oh come on, Papa Duck, let's wash up and go to dinner."

"Love you, Mama Duck," he said, eyes watering.

"Love you too, Papa Duck," she said, thinking how to make the room a bit homey.

They washed up and went to dinner at the Thunderbird Restaurant, which was larger and more crowded than Burbank had expected it to be. Which was good, for he liked people around him when he used his teeth, even if they were farmers eating out for the second or third time in a year, wearing their cardboard suits, their necks showing dirt in the creases, their hands overblown from field work, the nails horny, looking like things that had come out of the soil: onion grass, chickweed, forgotten bulbs discovered by a spade. And he enjoyed seeing other people use their teeth, seeing them flashing, hearing them strike bone on bone, especially if the teeth were lilywhite, bulging, gleaming like little pearly convex doors, lighting up a face with the beauty of power the way a bull's black hump lit up the head, horns: the ungleaming horns that dug into a man's groin, slicing, ripping, exposing flesh, bone. As for himself, he liked his meat almost raw, he had the hatchets for it, his teeth were magnificent and he knew it, so bulky they took up much of his jaw, pushing against his lips like packets of snuff (he remembered Southern black women with the snuff bulge behind their nether lip), with not a filling in them, rich with bite, teeth that for chomping and tearing he had never seen the equal of except in dogs, sharks, barracudas (he had reeled in barracudas in his time with pale triangular teeth set in jaws whose occlusion would have broken the heart of any orthodontist). What troubled him was the sight of gums doing the work that teeth ought to do, or wad-blackened, snuff-blackened teeth at work, or rotted, broken, stumpy, fragmented, pitted, caried teeth, although he had to confess to himself at times that the sight of such teeth struggling against meat did his heart good, reminding him of the magnificent cleavers the good Lord in his graciousness had seen fit to give him.

There were all kinds of space in this restaurant, recessing off into shadows, pretending to mystery where there wasn't the least bit of it. He had no doubt space was being used here inefficiently, but then it wasn't costly down here, which was one of the understatements of the decade. He knew Maryland, the Eastern Shore, many things places people, so many they were weighing him down. Or was the old noodle tiring for other reasons? Not that it wasn't a miracle he hadn't blown his fuse long, long ago, what with the shortcircuiting Mama Duck's heart had caused him, sexual and otherwise. Benign hypertrophy of the prostate, that's what he had. Too much semen backed up for too long. Anyway, he felt at home here, as he felt at home almost anywhere in the nation. In Mexico too, Chile, Peru, Colombia, Guatemala, you name it. He had been a partner in a Guatemalan sugar plantation and had developed (helped develop) it with his bare hands (poetically speaking). He had had (they had had) a fire there and won. He could still feel the flames. He remembered the sandbars, the shouting, the smell of sweat. He had sold out in time at a great profit. *His* ear was always to the ground. He had a barrel body and he got on tremendously with body people: peasants, fishermen, carpenters, blacksmiths. He had prided himself on going alone into the cane without a gun. It had meant a great deal to him that the natives had liked him. He had given them rum at fiesta time and had dived off his boat into shark-infested waters to show the kind of guts he had.

There would have been no trouble in the restaurant if Mama Duck hadn't brought her knitting along. The cashier, a faded old woman on a high chair behind a counter and a register, said tiredly, "Leave the bag there," and waved toward an ancient bench that might once have served as a pew. Ethel, frowning, made a move to set the bag down.

"You just hold on to that, hear?" Burbank said softly.

"Please let's not have any trouble," Ethel said.

"Where's the hostess?" he asked coldly, glaring at the cashier, who looked now like an oldfashioned beaded lamp, gray, tasseled, stupid.

The lamp wasn't bothered by his glare. The hostess came up, pressing some large shiny menus to her far-from-ample bosom.

"You mean to tell me my wife can't take her knitting bag to our table?" he asked.

The hostess resembled a pig with her little glinting eyes, a longfaced jaundiced sow who had spent too much time in labor.

Surveying him, she said, "That's right. It's the rule here."

"Get the manager."

"What for?"

"I have some sex jokes to tell him."

"Papa," Mrs. Burbank pleaded.

The hostess glanced sharply at him and retired to the rear of the place.

13

"Please, Papa Duck, we have trouble enough," Mrs. Burbank said.

She meant no doubt that *he* had trouble, and that his trouble was *her* trouble. His Emperor on the blink, he an alcoholic, prematurely retired. Maybe she was also thinking about her heart, and old age creeping in, and their kids scattered, and the loneliness and rot that were biting deep, like an acid.

"We don't *have* any trouble is the trouble," he said with a grunt, not bothering to look at her. What he meant was there was a hollowness in his life which only trouble could fill. Mrs. Burbank realized he had caught the manager's scent. "*Thunder-bird*," he said, tasting remembered bourbon on the sides of his thickening tongue.

A man entered the rear of the room and made his way toward them. Burbank turned a malevolent gaze on him, a feat that was easy inasmuch as the man was taller than he by some three or four inches. The man wore a tired charcoal suit, a tired white shirt and an exhausted black tie. But as he drew close, what advanced toward Burbank wasn't so much a face as large blue eyes that increasingly showed veins. Nor did they exhibit weakness. On the contrary, they showed a look of expected triumph. Burbank felt suddenly that his own position wasn't too secure. He was a transient, ignorant of the local laws, and his Emperor was sick, maybe *very* sick. The cool quartz eyes studied his carefully. They were out of character in the small, bony face. Strands of dead graying hair hugged the small, balding head as if glued to the skull.

But before the man could speak, Burbank said acidly, "I'm going to sue you for infringing my wife's personal rights. What's your name?"

He drew out a business card and a gold Montblanc pen.

"*We're* not infringing your wife's personal rights, my good sir," the man said quietly, smiling down at him.

"Your name, sir."

Burbank saw with pleasure that the man was beginning to flush.

"Let me explain. Sir, the—"

"I'm going to sue you, sir. Into the ground."

"Well, a lot of people make a living like this," the man said, still smiling.

Burbank glanced up sharply from the card.

"My good sir," he said slowly, "I'm going to sue this *restaurant* for invading my wife's personal rights, and I'm going to sue *you* for slander. *What's* your name? Or don't you have one?"

"Johnston, Philip, sir. Wait a minute."

Burbank wrote the name down and strode powerfully and coldly toward the door. The manager ran to cut him off, looking frightened.

"If you cool off, sir, I'll explain," he said huskily.

"After you apologize."

The man studied Burbank's eyes a moment, saw a demon of malevolence, and said, "I apologize."

"Louder," said Burbank, almost in a whisper.

"I apologize," the man said loudly, causing several diners to glance up and the cashier and the hostess to look shocked.

Burbank took his wife's arm and led her to a table in the middle of the room, the manager following. When the Burbanks were seated the manager, standing beside Burbank, asked, "Will you shake hands, sir?"

Burbank offered him a limp, cool hand.

"No hard feelings?"

Burbank grunted.

Philip Johnston stood solemn and tall and tears filled his eyes and threatened to overflow the lids.

"Sir," Johnston said, then was overcome for a moment. "Sir, I'm big enough to apologize and not hold a grudge and I'm big enough to accept an apology. I've had my ups and downs, bitter moments, you might say. I've had seven jobs and I'll probably have seven more. You see, sir, I'm a Catholic. Not that I'm against anybody—Protestants, Jews, Mohammedans. Live and let live, I say."

There was a pause.

"Happy Thanksgiving, sir. And you too, ma'am," Johnston said moistly.

"Happy Thanksgiving," Mrs. Burbank said.

"I hate bootlickers," Burbank said after Johnston departed.

"You always get what you want, don't you?" Ethel said.

"I do and I don't," he replied in a tired voice, surprising her.

He was disquieted by the fact that Johnston was a Catholic down here. Nothing was genuine anymore. Catholics posed as Protestants, Republicans voted Democrat, blacks got whiter and whiter.

The hostess had handed them menus. They were too large and slick for this village-idiot operation. When would the South stop trying to put on the dog? Have a look in the mirror, boys, squeeze the blackheads, cat the yeast until you foam at the mouth or you'll die sure as shooting of a case of the pimples.

"What'll you all have to drink?" the hostess asked carefully, trying not to look directly at them, as if they were evil, and frighteningly powerful, capable by means of tricks of law and words (the dangers that lay hidden in language!) of crushing her and hers.

"Four Jack Daniel's on the rocks," he said smoothly, as if he had been waiting for his cue.

"No no!" Mrs. Burbank cried. "He's joking!"

"Do I look like a joker?" he asked the hostess, his steely eyes glinting and his broad mouth spread in a thin smile. "Yes yes I am at that. Forget the stuff."

She replied with her own thin smile, still holding her clutch of menus against her tired breasts which even at the height of their power had let her down. In his opinion her smile fell entirely flat. After a moment she went off, head high, defiant. Not that it bothered him.

As the Burbanks studied the menu they were surprised by the festive atmosphere of the place. Newly gathered pumpkins here and there; paper decorations festooning the walls; three large mincemeat pies sitting on gleaming salvers on a table in the middle of the room; and a cornucopia spilling fruits and nuts. Naturally they ordered the turkey dinner. The word *turkey* brought visions of former dinners in the large brick house in Princeton, the children and grandchildren present. Lawns still green; trees bare except for the pines; starlings, redbreasts and sparrows feeding at their stations; a cardinal, high in a tree, singing its long full notes, then metallically twittering; chandeliers sprinkling an orange warmth; embroidered napkins, cut in the European style, heavy and gentle to the touch; onion-pattern Meissenware agleam; gold goblets heron-legged among the fat family silver; cranberry sauce, carbuncular and sweet, high in its mounds; plum pudding aflame. The word *turkey* also brought visions of the *Mayflower*. For Mrs. Burbank the *Mayflower* was a vessel on which an ancestor had come over, and Plymouth Rock was a stone, whereas for Burbank *Mayflower* was the Mayflower in D.C., where he had had some pretty good times, and Plymouth Rock reminded him of Plymouth gin.

Their waitress was tall, for which reason Burbank told himself to pity her, having long ago been informed by his wife (who was of optimum height) that tallness for a woman was as troublesome as shortness for a man. (She had added that *his* height suited her to a T.) He had always coveted tall gals, there was more leg to them, more belly, skedaddle. He made

17

up his mind to be pleasant to the waitress although her dubious accent grated on his ears. It also aroused his suspicion; it seemed to contain New Jersey notes. However, she made it hard for him to be pleasant, she avoided his face and missed the smile he was offering her and the glint in the eye, and there was something masculine about her that was like sandpaper to his soul. If there was one thing he hated it was masculine women. He wanted women to make him feel like the man he truly was, he liked his women frilly, soft, curvy, smelling of idleness and perfume and dressed in the latest fashion, with plenty of jewelry. Which was to say he liked the Southern gals, the kind he had grown up among, who twitched their spreading behinds, talked through their noses, arranged their hair with the lightest of fingertips and were professional females though he sure didn't care for the professional teaser every last one of them was. Still, he had married a Princeton gal who was all lady, bless her, and all guts.

The waitress had guts too, but when she challenged his right to eat what he pleased she made it mighty difficult for him to hang on to his temper, and he was convinced then that she was several years older than he had at first guessed, and harder and colder, and probably a sadsack in bed. When he said they would have the turkey dinner, specifying that *he* would have only *white* meat, she gave him a sidelong glance that said *she* knew where *he* came from, and *nobody* from *that* place had the standing of anybody from *this* one, regardless of how much dough they had, heading for Palm Beach and points south, or if they drove a customized Emperor—a customized Emperor, by the way, that was standing in the driveway like a wornout horse, head down, down, *down* in anguish and defeat, glad to be shielded by night, broken in heart and soul, waiting to be taken to the glue factory (images that stirred a terrible anguish in Burbank's chest). What did she *know?* Had the word got around? Had the tappet covers, those gleaming *things*, caused a sensation—gnashing of teeth, foaming at the mouth? She shook her curly head and he saw her eyes were almond-shaped. She said (with the effect somehow of a yawn, and her voice was hard, efficient, self-assured), "Sir, that ain't how we serve it here. There's dark and white on *every* plate." Which struck him as astounding coming from a Maryland gal, and made him wonder if she was a Commie or what.

"Are you all that integrated down here?" he asked, intending it as a light joke.

Her eyes froze and turned away. Now, he didn't care a hoot for women who turned their gaze away from his, callously, angrily, not if they were serving him, dependent on him, like his daughters, secretaries, this gal here, who in a little while would be looking for a fat Thanksgiving Day tip. Lucky for her it was the Day of Thanksgiving. He only stared at her, a long hard stare, the kind that penetrated skull, with an extremely thin smile playing over his broad mouth, emphasizing how close-shaven his broad upper lip was. Then he said softly, nasally, "I don't care *how* it's served."

"Oh. All right then," she responded, mistaking his drift.

"Just bring me white meat like a good gal," he said evenly, but the steel had edged its way into his voice.

"I *told* you, sir," she said, and she couldn't help glancing forlornly toward the kitchen, where no doubt Philip Johnston, good Catholic, was observing him through a peephole. It occurred to Burbank then that her tallness was as disfiguring as a harelip.

"Papa Duck," Ethel said softly, leaning forward and frowning. But her tone was too soft, almost a whisper, and she had made the mistake of looking uneasily around. He reacted with the pleasure of a fire graced by a sprinkling of kerosene.

"Heck, bring me *two* dinners," he said, increasing his decibels and drawling a little. "Or three. Or four. Just bring me enough dinners to add up to some *white* meat. I don't want miscegenation on my plate."

Again he meant this as a joke. Again the waitress stiffened, as if he had said a fourletter word. He knew by instinct how a New Yorker should handle an obstreperous Maryland hick.

"Papa Duck," Ethel said, trying to catch his eye.

But his steely eye, much like Nuncle's, was fastened on the waitress's. If there was one thing he knew as well as Nuncle it was the functioning of the pecking order.

"*Sir*," the gal said.

"Is there anything you all got against my ordering four all-American dinners?" he wanted to know.

"No sir."

"Well that's what I want."

"Four *whole* dinners?"

"Heck no!" he responded with a small, preliminary explosion. This Eastern Shore gal was really shoving him. "Just. Four. Orders. Of all-American turkey."

"And what'll I do with the rest?"

"Throw it on the floor and step on it," he said dryly.

She stared, then laughed in a hesitant way. She had had no experience, apparently, in dealing with a man of his caliber. "Yes sir," she finally said, and did just what he had asked her to do—that is, brought four. orders. of turkey. But she was too sensible a gal to throw good food on the floor, much less step on it. He presented one order to Mama Duck, gathered the white meat from the other three onto one plate and had the waitress remove the excess.

"You have to fight all the way," he remarked to Ethel after the gal had left.

"*You* do, Papa Duck," Ethel said.

He glared at her.

"If you mean that as a compliment I agree," he said gently, eyes shining, and she let it go at that.

"Well, we have much to be thankful for," she said to change the subject.

"You can bet your bottom dollar," he said, tearing into a mass of meat and eyeing her steadily. "And don't forget the money. Where'd we be if it weren't for mah money?"

He had unaccountably slipped into a dialect.

"Yes yes yes yes yes," she said, looking through him.

"How'd you like it if I drove off and *left* you here?" he asked.

"In what? That brokendown jalopy?"

She truly astonished him at times. There was something in this good woman that wouldn't go down, some great good spirit that ought to be handsomely rewarded. He opened his eyes as wide as he could and bit down with all his might, risking chipping a tooth on bone. She expected him to say something stunning, outrageous, but he only laughed, showed his powerful, gleaming, overlapping teeth, his eyes warming and shrinking, and muttered almost genially, "What gets into you? Coming along and cramping my style?"

"Yes yes yes," she said.

He wiped his mouth. "I'd get me a gal in Acapulcuh and have me a whale of a time if I didn't have *you* along." Again there was a trace of a Southern accent.

"Why don't you then?" she responded in sudden anger, eyes glowing with hatred.

It did his heart good to see this honest venomous look, which brought back a comforting sense of reality. But he had sense enough to quit, for he didn't want to risk her having an attack down here among rednecks, plop in the middle of nowhere.

When they finished dinner they left promptly, as if they

had stopped only briefly and were going to drive the rest of the night. A couple of drivers were entering their cars. He listened for the sounds: starter, engine, then the cars driving off, leaving him behind. He wanted so badly to take off. For what was an American if he wasn't on the *go?* Ethel, poor creature, knew just what to do: she turned on the TV and settled herself into a chair. He too watched the screen awhile, then fell asleep.

He dreamed he and she each had a car. They were parked on a San Francisco hill. Their brakes failed, and both cars rolled downhill and smashed into parked cars, causing explosions. But miraculously no one was hurt. Then he was visiting his mom's apartment, a condominium, and outside the living room was a strange puddle, and the shoreline was irregular, and the building began to list, it was about to become a new Leaning Tower, and cracks appeared like arrows in the walls, and it seemed they (mother and son) would be crushed, and then, thank God, the building found a balance. Now he was in his own apartment, which had fifteen rooms and which he shared not only with Ethel but with their children and grandchildren. He was in the master bedroom when he discovered to his stupefaction that it had been turned into a dorm! He shouted at Ethel with all his might, demanding to know why she had done this. He shouted until he was hoarse. The worst of it was that everybody was not only sleeping in the master bedroom but cooking, eating! Meanwhile Ethel was immaculate, her fingernails gleamed with fresh polish, and she was wearing elegant shoes with stylish heels, and she was rational, cool. She looked perplexed, wondering why he was on the verge of losing his mind over something so trivial.

"Christopher," a voice said gently.

It was Mama Duck, rousing him to turn in for the night.

He undressed and got into bed without brushing his teeth though he was a conscientious tooth brusher. He would brush them an extra time tomorrow. It would help fill the emptiness of the coming day, or what his sense of his destiny told him would be the emptiness.

BURBANK WASN'T THE MAN TO WASTE TIME next morning. Opening his eyes, he was at once in the land of the living. He sat up suddenly, padded to one of the large draped windows and unbuttoned his pajama top to give his ample, hairless chest a chance to taste the Eastern Shore air. He pushed aside the nappy, burnt-sienna, dust-smelling drapes and peered out. Motel night, with a winking of weak electric bulbs.

Knucklehead came over and licked his hand, making his morning skin crawl. Why did he always have somebody on his back? He said gruffly but mutedly, "Lie down!" and Flora, sensing his mood, obeyed. It had been a pro forma lick anyway, with the intention of warding off the day's evil. He thrust his short but powerful arms into a maroon dressing gown and went outside, still barefoot.

There the Emperor was, just standing there, all-American though it was. He had once felt affection for it. Now he felt shame, contempt, as if it were a Datsun or a VW or a Subaru or a Toyota (not that he put much stock in the BMW, the Mercedes, the Volvo, the Saab—or, for that matter, the Alfa Romeo, the Jaguar, the . . . you name it). He tried to start the engine but nothing happened. Not that he had expected anything. Not that he was a pessimist this Eastern Shore morning. But somehow he thought he knew the sound of finality, somehow he thought he had heard it as he had rolled down the Eastern Shore hill. If the customized, gleaming, beautifully oiled Emperor engine had burst into its usual purring muffled roar what a great day this would have been, so different from the one that had just begun! The only sound was the turning of the gold key in its casing. Nothing stirred at this close-to-dawn, Eastern Shore morning.

He returned to the room. Mama Duck was asleep on her side. Knucklehead lifted her head to glance at him (she was always checking him out, as if he couldn't be trusted). Nuncle scissored briefly and was still. There was a noise in the plumbing as if somebody was beginning the day. Very well: the Eastern Shore night had ended even though the sky was still black. Having reached this conclusion, Burbank proceeded at once to act on it. He went to the shower, peeled off his pajamas, let lukewarm water flood his back and chest, soaped himself, then rinsed himself with water as cold as the time and place afforded, and this despite what one doctor had warned: that such a vascular change at his age wasn't wise. Burbank, however, had his own opinions, and if his kids, particularly the girls, found him dogmatic, *he* found *them* wishywashy, and anyhow *he* got things *done*. What was more, he footed the bills.

He dressed, went outside and paced up and down. The Emperor's present condition sickened him, it made him lust for a couple of snorts. He went to the car and glared at it, as if by glaring he could frighten it into submission. It wasn't that kind of car, however. It was, after all, an Emperor, and a customized one at that. An occasional car sped up or down the highway, long lights making the countryside look ghostly and awaking a great envy in him. Two motel guests emerged and drove off in a burst of exhaust fumes after letting their morning-sleepy eyes glance off him and their headlights blind him. Still no sign of life in the garage, and the restaurant was still closed. CRACKERS ALL! What was he to do? There was all this *time*. Floating behind the wheel of the Emperor at ninety, heading for the Keys and the lust heat of the beaches, he had had the world by the balls. Now he had time, or rather time had *him*.

He got bored, so he went inside and sat in an armchair and thought of nothing . . . nothing, that is, except for his recent meeting with George Forman, whom he hadn't seen for only a couple of years, but what a *change* in old George! Luckily he had learned in advance that old George was failing, so he had been able to brace himself a bit, but even so it had been a hell of a shock. He recalled his first view of old George at that last meeting: at a distance: outdoors: old George still tall, but bent now, somehow small, and with very careful, very hesitant steps, as if life had busted all his arches for him, or ripped off everything except the nerve ends. His face was smaller, too. And he carried his hands in front of him like hurt birds, and they were shaking funnily. And he had trouble speaking (old George): the words seemed to stick in his Adam's apple, letting his lips whisper away without them, or they rushed past his lips before the lips had a chance to get moving. Poor old George had stripped his gears. And the nether lip, which hadn't seemed large to Burbank before, now spoke insistently. Thicker, broader, bluish under the false lowers that were too neat, too small, too white (with a bluish cast). Burbank was careful not to stare, but the lip intruded: heavy, coarse, symbolizing what had happened, was happening. Poor old George, whom he had camped with in the high country. George who could outclimb anybody, and outcarry too. George with the folded boat on his back, leaping between rocks in the high-country stream with the fool's gold glinting in it. With his height that never bothered Burbank because he was such a naturally good guy. His back looking warm, hard, decent as he squatted over a fire. The nether lip kept signaling to Burbank—at lunch, on the terrace. It was an extremely intense and intelligent signal. And in the house poor old George bending painfully to get a grip on the old cat and three or four times the old cat sauntering away from under that attempted laying on of bony, long-fingered, scaly hands. A mourning dove cooing somewhere. Old George with the great long levers of arms and the wiry hands that had gripped an ax handle, a saddle. His face mask-like, his lips twitching before the "Anna" came out. And Anna behaving as if everything was normal, her hair still blond although muddy now with gray. The heat foaming under the beamed ceiling, billowing, massive, and old George and Anna claiming you got used to it. Mama Duck with her brown eyes a little glazed, and moisture on the down of her lip, and breathing heavily, and her speech slowing down, thickening (what was the altitude? two thousand? three?), and he, Burbank, thinking of the oxygen tank in the car. Outside: thin woods, dry ground, placer mining hill, rock garden. And far away, misted over, furry mountains. And old George's hands . . . the hurt birds.

Burbank went outside to stop the flow of these thoughts.

The restaurant now showed lights (if you could call them that; he judged they were sixty-watters). Crossing the broad driveway backed by rolling wornout fields and distant stands of scraggly timber, and opening the door, he recalled with a twinge that his Emperor was unwell, and the feeling of unease that crept up his powerful legs made him hesitate about going inside. But he plunged in as though he had been shot out of a cannon, which was the only way to enter these dumps. The festive atmosphere was gone. The place felt hollow, cold. He had ham and eggs. The ham was hard, salty, the eggs powdery. The waitress, whom he didn't recognize, asked, "Everything okay?' A philosophical kind of question if you cared to look at it a certain way. He could have told her what he thought of it, as well as what he thought of the cooking, but it being only a day after the Day of Thanksgiving he restrained himself.

He stepped outside. There were signs of life in the garage: lights and the movement of human figures. He crossed the highway. As though to greet him, a tow truck emerged from the garage and headed toward him. He stepped aside to let it pass, not recognizing the driver. But instead of passing him it stopped beside him, and he saw that the driver was gazing at him curiously. Then he realized it was John Carradine, looking more cadaverous than ever, and he had a start. He hadn't expected to meet John Carradine again so soon, although he couldn't have said why. But there the cracker was, regarding him not only from his naturally greater height but from the infinitely superior height of the truck's cab. Which wasn't exactly calculated to make Burbank do a jig of triumph this Eastern Shore morning. Yet Burbank was solid if he was anything, he was all meat and guts, he was a Georgie Patton and he knew it. If you were one of the people in this world who were allowed to clap him on the back you struck rock, nothing less, whereas John Carradine clearly was not long for this world. Burbank started to say something but his throat was rusty, which was what came of starting the day without a couple of shots.

"Morning," Carradine said at last, smiling faintly, and Burbank didn't appreciate the thinness of the smile, being a thin smiler himself. Also, the rumbling of the truck's engine was offensive, a guttural, snarling-animal sound. Still, there was life in it, which Burbank couldn't deny, whereas his own engine was perhaps mortally silent despite its high tech. However, if the Emperor resembled a hearse because of its black lacquer and trim (almost all the exterior chrome had been covered by lacquer at Burbank's direction) this didn't bother him one whit, for he had sent many people into the hereafter (figuratively speaking) and had done so with considerable and efficient pleasure. It occurred to him that Carradine was behaving more like a Down-Easter than a Southerner and Burbank didn't appreciate it. But it was time to answer the man.

"When are you going to do something about my Emperor?" he asked dryly.

"Right now," Carradine drawled, and once again Burbank didn't like the way the words were spoken in the man's nose and once more the drawl, like a sea wind, menaced him. There was just one thing to do under the circumstances and he did it: leaped into the cab and plopped down on the scuffed seat. It did him good to study the man's look of surprise followed by a glance of dawning respect. Burbank was no mean adversary, and it was well for him that Carradine grasped that drift. If Carradine thought that because he was on native soil he was going to push Burbank around he had another and surprising thought coming, for one of the things that distinguished Burbank in this world was that he attached himself to no particular piece of real estate, he was no tinhorn, no big fish in a little pond, he was not only on golfing friendships with the greats and near-greats of this world, he was one of the near-greats himself and could pull plenty of strings wherever he happened to find himself.

It was clear that Carradine gathered all this or a reasonable facsimile thereof, yokel that he was notwithstanding, for he said not a word and turned his gaze away from Burbank's and drove across the highway to the stricken Emperor. He climbed down, fetched a chain and went to attach it to the rear end. But Burbank, being a front-end man, didn't approve of this bass-ackwardness, so he leaned out of the cab and said grittily, "Tow her forwards." This was a mistake that he wouldn't have made if he had been in his cups, for when in his cups he was a more sensible man than when he was sober. Carradine grumbled something and eyed Burbank with that cool enamel gaze that the first man had turned on him at yesterday's twilight. "Hm," Burbank grunted, not understanding what Carradine had said but realizing enough to know he had best let go of the subject. He leaned back, conscious of the spread inside him of the virus of defeat, nourished so readily by his sobriety. Carradine cranked the Emperor's rear end off the ground and they took off, climbing a couple of hills and coming to a stretch of highway construction. Then they were in a village: bleak, damp, lying on one side of the highway. They turned left and drove up a street and into a garage, where John Carradine descended and spoke to a cracker named Jud.

Jud was the only word Burbank could make out, for Carradine lowered his voice and leaned toward Jud's ear. But Burbank noticed that Carradine had failed to glance *his* way but that Jud did, furtively. Even at that distance he could see that Jud was flushing under the impact of what Carradine was telling him, and he was alerted to some new trouble he was going to have on his hands, now in this Eastern Shore place called Yazoo. Carradine retrieved his chain and asked for ten bucks. Burbank gave him fifteen, much to the man's and Jud's surprise. Then Carradine drove off while Burbank braced himself to deal with the newest cracker situation.

Jud was in no hurry to attend to Burbank's wants. He apparently assumed that Burbank had as much time on his hands as *he* had. After a fleeting glance at Burbank he disappeared into an office, leaving Burbank to debate whether to follow him and demand immediate action or to stay put until his temper cooled. He decided on the latter course although it graveled him to do so. He would square matters with Jud later. Standing beside the Emperor's hood, Burbank now sensed it wasn't only Jud who regarded time in this way but the garage itself, with its dimness, dirt, cobwebs and smell of rotting pine. Time seemed to be caked on the walls, on the windowpanes, to loom over the old truck squatting on its axles, over the sedan with a gaping front end, and over the coupe with its rear on jacks, the transmission missing. Time was everywhere: palpable, cheap, frozen. There was so much of it in this air it seemed to Burbank now to have no value whatsoever. He thought he heard Jud's voice in the office: subdued, explanatory, wheedling. When Jud appeared, Burbank turned his steely gaze pointblank on him.

Jud came so close he caught Burbank offguard momentarily and said in a voice that was surprisingly hearty and confident, "Yes *suh*. *Whut* kin we do you for, sir?"

"You can do something for my *Emperor*," Burbank corrected.

"Yes *suh*, Mr. Burbank."

"How you know my name?"

"They called to say you were coming."

"They? You mean that Johnston?" The corner of Burbank's mouth twitched once.

"Yes *suh*. Tain't every day an *Emperor* rolls along down here."

"You the foreman?"

"Yes *suh*. Jud James, suh. Whut seems to be the trouble, Mr. Burbank?"

"The trouble *seems* to be that my Emperor's on the blink, Mr. James, *sir*," Burbank said, then, in the same tone, explained what had happened. Mr. James nodded occasionally to show that the information was taking hold. "*Well* now," he said when Burbank finished. It was human of Burbank to assume that his Emperor would be attended to now, but he was wrong, for Mr. James, big man in Yazoo, returned to the office and stayed there almost ten minutes by Burbank's wafer-thin gold wristwatch.

Which gave Burbank an opportunity to reflect further on the value set on time in Yazoo, as well as to observe the garage more closely. It was little more than a shed, with an old hoist suspended from a ceiling beam and with a beatup ventilator not in use. It was clear the floor was rarely cleaned—there were old puddles of oil, chunks of grease, nodules of sand, and dirt and bleakness everywhere. No sign of hydraulic lifts or of pits. There *was* a dimness and a biting cold.

Jud James reappeared, wearing his blue felt hunting cap with the earflaps. He was slim, taller than Burbank, and showed a soft vague smile of false teeth. His coloring was fair. His cheeks seemed to show down. He turned the Emperor's ignition key. Silence answered him. He fetched a battery, connected it to the Emperor's battery. When he turned the gold key again the Emperor set up such a thunder he winced, flushed and let go as if the key was red-hot. Burbank's fingertips flinched and his feet went very cold. Jud James called over the man working on the sedan: a pale, small, fragile guy named Smith, whom Burbank immediately and silently named Spineless George. Spineless George walked stiff-kneed over to his boss and gazed at him with listless eyes and a red slit of a mouth in a greasy face, his hair dead on his head and he dead on his feet. Burbank wondered if that stiff-kneed walk could be caused by the stiffness of the jeans he wore, for the grease had set hard in them now that late fall had come. His shoes were so grease-covered they had no color, his hands were black with it, his shirt, once white, was starched with it. Even so, Burbank couldn't understand how the man kept his body heat in the place, he being so thin and the doors being open to the fall air.

After studying Jud's face and apparently finding it as empty as Burbank had, Spineless George turned his attention to the Emperor, staring at the engine with its blazing chrome. For all the phoning that had taken place about it, it was clear he had been kept in the dark, for he leaned forward as if he mistrusted his eyeballs and asked with a tone of resentment, "Whut's *at* fur?" addressing not Burbank but Jud James. Old Jud, flushing, leaned forward, possibly to have the black hood between himself and Burbank.

"Whut's at *fur?*" Spineless George insisted. He was no doubt referring to the name on the tappet covers. It was pathetic to see him looking up at the taller Jud James.

Old Jud said, "Check the compression."

Spineless George, shorter than Burbank, his eyes dead, his hair dead, his teeth bad, his skin an electric blue, checked the compression with a hand meter. When he had finished the last of the twelve cylinders, Jud told him to return to the sedan, which he did with his stiff-kneed walk. Then Jud, wearing a light hunting jacket, an old white shirt and moccasins, slid under the Emperor on a wheeled platform and began to remove its pan. By this time Burbank, gut wilting, was pacing the cement apron of the short driveway.

Deciding it was more than time he cleared his head, he crossed the street and entered a drugstore, where he bought a bottle of breath sweetener. Thank God for Mama Duck! His eyes misted at the thought of her. Where'd he be without her?

In the gutter, no doubt. And thank God for breath sweeteners as well as for the drugstores that sold them even on the dusty streets of the Yazoos of this world! Poor old Ethel! Oxygen tank in the bedroom; array of pills; easily winded; fainting spells; heart pounding at the slightest exertion! All because the valve, scarred by rheumatic fever, let only a trickle of blood through. Three open-heart operations. Silvertooth, the surgeon, calling her Lion-Hearted. And she planning her funeral down to the smallest details. Aortic valve reamed, muscle sutured, and soon she was up and about again, climbing stairs, helping the maids, spending nights at high altitude to accompany him on some of his trips—Peru, for example. Eyes fatigued, skin sallow, flaccid, thin legs swollen. Burbank thought of the Keys. Gingerbread houses; banyan, jacaranda and frangipani trees; oleander, hibiscus, ixora. Yellowtails; silver snappers; red groupers. He remembered a huge barracuda, with its cavernous mouth, protruding lower jaw, sunwashed teeth, large round staring eye.

He returned to the garage, saw a small faded sign proclaiming it was the Edward Garage, and encountered Jud James, who, looking guilty, said in a low, furtive voice, "You've got a bad rod bearing."

"You're wrong," Burbank instantly retorted. "My *Emperor* may have a bad rod bearing. It's *you* who may have a bad bearing." And he smiled thinly with the pleasure of his wit, so that Jud James, like the waitress of yesterday, sensed the strong teeth under the stretched broad mouth.

"Suh?" Jud asked, blinking short lashes.

"Skip it," Burbank said.

Jud flushed. Burbank thereupon knew he had hit nerve tissue and that Jud James was flesh and blood although Burbank might not have thought so on first encounter. One of the reasons for Burbank's success in life was his habit of turning resolutely away from everything distasteful to him, regardless of cause or effect, right or wrong. He could turn away as easily as an insect encountering a wrong scent. It was this application of an insect principle to a type of human behavior that had given him so clear an advantage in the struggle upward.

"Fix it," he said suddenly, harshly. "That's what you're here for, isn't it? Or is it?"

Jud James, a delicate figure of an Eastern Shore guy, possibly feeling himself milk-muscled compared with Burbank's elderly brawn, cast his eyes down. Apparently they were too heavy to stand up to Burbank's vigorous ones. He wasn't used to an Emperor man.

"Trouble is, suh," he said stumblingly, apologetically, "we got to inspect your shaft, to see if *hit's* okay."

"Don't you all go questioning *my* shaft," said Burbank sternly.

"We *got* to inspect it, suh," Jud said in a lower tone, and the long fingers of his right hand brushed like feathers across his boyish mouth.

"Well get going then! Who's the owner here?"

"Mist Edward stepped out."

"Well *I'm* stepping out, and when I get back I aim to chat with him! You tell him that!"

"Yes *suh*," said Jud, feeling the futility of arguing with real dough.

"Bright boy," Burbank said, eyes agleam, and he exited, head swimming.

But he had taken no more than twenty paces when Jud James called out, "Mr. Burbank! Here's Mist Edward his very sef!"

Turning, Burbank saw Mist Edward standing beside James in the driveway, smiling and waving to him as if they were blood brothers. But Mist Edward was sadly mistaken, for Burbank wasn't that readily a blood brother of anybody's, even in the fair and friendly world of banking, much less in this Yazoo down here. Burbank advanced toward Mist Edward with the resolute step of a man with ample experience of testing his opponent's mettle. The most conspicuous and pleasant thing about Mist Edward, he judged at a distance, was that his height was almost precisely that of Burbank himself. When Burbank came abreast of him, Mist Edward, grinning, held out a meaty hand and said, "Most tremenjous pleasure to meet a man of *your* caliber, Mr. Burbank!"

"Likewise," Burbank said softly, ironically, glancing not into Mist Edward's eyes but into the thick lenses of the dark glasses he wore, which in motion gave Burbank glimpses of the fall sky. It was a disadvantage to Burbank not to be able to focus his gaze on his opponent's and he felt it.

"Ah understand you all want to talk to me," Mist Edward said. "Will you be so kind then as to step into mah leetle bitsy office?"

The office was clean, to Burbank's surprise. Mist Edward closed the thin windowed door between it and the garage, reaching behind Burbank to do so.

"Caint be too careful bout the hep listenin in," he explained.

Burbank, relaxing, smiled the kind of genial smile that came over him when treachery was afoot. Still, he had a few points to make and he intended to make them flat out.

"Mist Edward," he began, "you may have some of the finest experience in this world in tinkering with Fords and Chevies, but can you make an Emperor that's in some kind of trouble *work?* Because it isn't Eastern Shore guts that's needed, it's expertise. Where's your *expertise?* I tell you this because I have a certain affection for my Emperor. As for attorneys, I retain a bunch of guys whose specialty is taking nobodies in noplaces and breaking their backs—CRACK!: so! At my signal they'd

come swarming into this Yazoo like a bunch of tree worms—
and armed with Eastern Shore law, none of that civil rights
stuff. So if you'd care to recommend an outfit that can do a
proper job on my Emperor, I invite you to do so."

Mist Edward, standing behind a beatup brown desk with
his knuckles on it, pressed his hands down hard, making the
knuckles crack. But the sound didn't frighten Burbank, nor
the sudden glare that flashed from Mist Edward's specs due
to a brittle movement of his head.

"Do you mind if Ah git you a dusty old chair?" Mist Edward
asked. "These leetle chitchats are *so* much more to the point
when good folks like yoursef take the trouble to *set*."

And he reached into a closet for a folding chair brittle and
faded with age, Burbank meanwhile surveying him more
closely. He was bald, his face was jovial and chunky, with a
thin mouth and a button nose, and his voice was high. He was
dressed in a blue suit, white shirt and a blue tie with a putter
printed on it.

Having opened the chair, he said with a flourish of his arm,
"Hit's a real *pleasure* to jaw with a man of your quality, suh.
May Ah shake your hand agin?"

Burbank accepted the hand thrust out at him, a butcher's
hand, the nails horny, the cuticles raw and thick, the flesh the
color of raw meat.

"*Now* then, suh," Mist Edward said, having seated himself
behind the desk, "*that* is the way Ah like to hear a man talk!
That's the way a *real* man talks, and Lordy knows real men
are dyin out fast, givin way to mealymouths and cottonmouths
an the like. But first let me say this: *that* is one honey of an
Emperor. Man, Ah *like* power! Bar, refrig, TV, phone! All
you need now is a lil ole swimmin pool!"

And he threw his head back and laughed with the pleasure

of contemplating Burbank's Emperor glory. Burbank, sitting down, slapped his thigh, laughed and tried to imagine a swimming pool enclosed in his Emperor.

"An Ah ain't even atalkin bout the injin," Mist Edward said in amazement. "Mah mother's soul, may she rest in peace! *That* is about as fur as we kin go, Mr. B," he said solemnly, his voice having assumed a sepulchral tone. "Now looka here. Ah'm gonna talk turkey to you. Ah caint *tell* you how sorry Ah am to witness a man of your quality demeaned by a *gar*age like mine. Hit's a downright shame for an Emperor to be hobnobbin with those filthy junk heaps. Lord, whut'll we see next? An that filth! But you see, Mr. Burbank, hit is im-*poss*ible for us to intro*duce* much less *maintain* Yank cleanliness an ef-*fee*shunsy. The hep wouldn't stand for it an Yazoo would be inflamed by it. An Ah tell *you* they are a bunch of *arsonists* when it come to local politics. But let me say this above all else, suh: this the *oney gar*age in Yazoo. Let me repeat mahsef: *oney*. You git mah drift? Ah know how you all feel, seein all that filth, grit, grease, bits of steel messin with oil. Krr! Makes a man grind his pore ole molars, don't it though? Don't it? Agree, Mr. B, *agree!* But whut you gonna *do?* Now you tell me that!"

"Come to the POINT," said Burbank sternly. "The POINT!"

"The point?" asked Mist Edward, and paused as if bewildered for a moment. "Why, the point's this. We get every kind of breakdown there is, from wheels flyin off at a hundred an ten to shorts that don't take more in half hour to set straight. From air in the fuel line, water in the gas tank, ole gummy plugs, busted hoses, steerin wheels that have come plum off an *killed* folks, brakes that have jammed an *murdered* gentle people, to busted axles, slipped clutches, chewed-up trans-*mee*shuns. Heck, Mr. B, you all want me to continue? As for wrecks, Ah won't demean your ears. Course, that's why they're always afixin the road an graftin an all. Theng is, folks don't *want* safety, an that's whut's so good for mah ole business. Heck, safety would put us all in the pore house in Yazoo. So when you come to think of it, *your* trouble is *no* trouble—yet. Still, Ah feel deeply for you, suh, cause if there's trouble that's *real* trouble, hit's your shaft goin bust, an it looks to me like hit's gone and done just that. But Ah kin see you're a man that knows how to take a lil of the bad with all the blessed good, God hep us every one, rich an pore alike."

"*That*, sir, is where you're mighty wrong," Burbank said crisply. "Ah don't know whut you're gittin at an Ah don't care."

He drew a sharp breath. It wouldn't do to slip into a Southern dialect at this crucial moment of his life even though his tongue was itching to do so.

"Mist Edward, let me make myself plain. I'd be more than happy to spend double the cost of my Emperor—no, make that triple—suing anybody who through ignorance or what*ever* makes mah Emperor onhappy. An that's all Ah have to say to you."

Burbank almost bit his lip with vexation over the dialect. Mist Edward cracked his knuckles in anguish against the desk top, mouth drooping in astonishment.

"Why, you haven't been alistenin to a theng Ah've said!" Mist Edward cried. "Suh, we don't always have us a choice in this life—that's *mah* drift. This is *Yazoo*, Mr. B. Why, consider mah windows. They have gone an got themselves an accumulation of twenty years of dirt, dust, grease n filth a livin! Ah haven't *dared* clean em. Why, there are spiders on some of em would make a spiderologist's eyeballs fall outa his bean. *Kin* Ah git rid of em? Ah kin *not*. The hep wouldn't stan for it! Con-sider mah equipment. You think the hep would let me git new stuff? Ah got to practically ax their per-meeshun to take me a piss, Mr. B! But whut's a man like me to do in Yazoo? Whut kin *you* do? Because, suh, we're in the same boat, swamp n founder alike."

"Mist Edward," Burbank said, "I'm going to my motel to have some lunch. When I return, I trust you'll have a better solution to my Emperor's problem than you've so far given me. Understand me? Now, are there cabs in this Yazoo?"

Mist Edward didn't reply. His glasses, because of the position of his head, had lost their glare. Burbank had the sense Mist Edward's eyes were closed with grief. Burbank left the office feeling he wasn't in the same condition as when he had entered it. It was as if a gas leak had secretly poisoned him.

HE HITCHHIKING! WHAT WERE THINGS COMING to? But having decided on this course of action, he strode to the highway to take up the necessary position. About a dozen cars, mostly foreign, ignored him except for two that sounded their horns and slowed down, only to accelerate in a burst of exhaust. *Action!* But how to get it now that his Emperor, like poor Ethel, was on the blink? If only his shaft turned out to be okay! But maybe like himself it had been prematurely retired.

He had been in deep trouble at the bank. Too many absences, latenesses, too much loose jaw and furry talk, too many lapses of memory, too many visits to dryingout places (known to McKenna, the board, the vice presidents, all the barracudas, a considerable number of whom had their own vulnerable spots). He had taken to doing odd things, stealing a guest towel at a McKenna party, a German beerhall ashtray from the Murdocks. And there was always McKenna, board chairman, keeping a round barracuda eye on him, debating when to ax him. The bank's offices were on lower Broadway, with terrific views of the harbor. McKenna's office was tremendous. Cream sofas and armchairs, cream rug, telescope, microscope, easel, atlases, globes, imitation fireplace crammed with cylinders of blueprints. McKenna was five years his senior, a Fordham grad, didn't drink, smoke, fornicate. Gray cheeks, round shoulders, barracuda mouth. Had a surplus of height, so he walked with a stoop to sample the air of more democratic altitudes. Teeth buck, with a gap between the two upper central incisors. Now how could Burbank trust a psalm-singing, foot-washing, total-immersion Catholic like that? No doubt the feeling was reciprocated, yet he and McKenna had spent years working successfully together—until the tolerance had thinned out like overheated oil. After which Burbank had felt spied on like any lesser executive.

The bank had the resources for both domestic and overseas spying. For example, there was this Mrs. McGee, a middle-aged lady in Rome (Catholic, fiercely religious). One morning, after a visit to St. Peter's, she went to a department store, rummaged around in expensive clothes, had fittings (but nothing suited her) and said some unfortunate things (like "Drop dead" and "Button your lip") to the English-speaking lady clerks, then ran out of the dressing room naked, grabbed expensive stuff off the counters and stomped on it, screaming. A bank spy gone bats. Her husband had dropped dead of a heart attack on a Westbury street a couple of years back. No kids. And so her honeymoon with the bank ended abruptly in a straitjacket in a Rome hospital. Burbank's had ended in . . .

There was this show in Miami Beach and he was with this gal he had met at the bar who was originally from Columbus, and she said she adored Miami but had no use for Miami Beach. What was she doing in Miami *Beach* then? Oh, the friend she was going to meet had come down with a bleeding ulcer, and she wouldn't consider marrying anybody who tried to take her away from Miami, felt more her*self* in Miami, had been in Miami, the love of her life, five months now, had been married to a traveling salesman (church furniture) who as a child in Arkansas had had asthma and been taken to a layer-on of hands who had given him a patent medicine containing arsenic, as it turned out, so his gonads had been damaged and he couldn't produce sperm. But she told him she loved his not making sperm, because she didn't want kids anyhow and it meant she didn't have to use birth control, but he accused her of screwing around because he wasn't a big sperm producer, and when they busted up she came to Miami. This kind of monologue convinced Burbank she needed to have her ashes hauled.

Aware of spotlights, orchestra music, onstage dancing, a display of tremendous breasts, some partially covered by costume jewelry, others bare except for the nipples, which were shielded by scintillating silver stars, he ordered a double bourbon on the rocks. In one number the gals wore, in addition to G-strings and stars, long white gloves, spike heels and a headdress of white pineapple-shaped feather sprays. They were attended by tight-assed gents in formfitting white suits with pink vests. He had kept ordering bourbon. . . . Anyhow, he had unzipped his fly and exposed himself and there had been several flashes of light from a bank spy's camera. A confrontation with McKenna in New York, a signature, a quiet resignation. No hard feelings. He would have done the same to McKenna.

Lo if it wasn't Mist Edward himself strolling to the highway now, observing his state of shame through the dark, glittering glasses.

"You all kin *stay* here, Mr. B, but it don't mean you're gonna *git* anywhere," Mist Edward said. "Lessen some sweet sympathetic soul'll come along an pick you up outa your pore misery. Seen it often, bigtimed folks, wads a green thickenin their pockets, standin lonely as kin be. Enough to make mah eyes water. Cause we done *had* it, suh, you an me."

Here Mist Edward felt his groin through the cloth of his old trousers—a good, solid feel, the way Southerners knew how to do better than anybody else in the country.

"Ah'll tell you *one* theng, though," he continued. "There's nothin old about me down *here*. Ah'm crazy bout goin out *into* sex. Sex is *life*. Hit's the greatest theng in the world to go out *into* sex! That's most of the story, except when you git too old. Good luck on catching yourself a lift, you hear? An by the way, you jist might want to calm yourself with a drink at Shorty's."

"Shorty's?" Burbank asked, caught by surprise.

"Why, right there on the rise."

And Mist Edward turned away and headed toward his garage. Burbank climbed the rise to Shorty's, which was an old converted frame house with a big sign. He entered it. In the middle of the low-ceiling smoky room was a square bar around which some men in work clothes were sitting on stools. The barkeep, frowning heavily (he was staring out of deep eye sockets and his pinched brow seemed to be telegraphing pain), was pouring a customer a Haig. His apron reached to his ankles. The whisky island in the bar's center was cluttered with pickled sausages, fried bacon rinds, hardboiled eggs, cheese twirls, onion chips, corn chips, chitterlings, barbecued potato chips.

Seating himself on a stool near the door, Burbank stared at the bartender. This was no man whose goodwill he cared about. This was a naught who leaned too far forward when he walked and who was round-shouldered and flat-chested. In addition, his forehead was too pale, there were cords in his nape, and his heavy-bearded, close-shaven face was very gaunt.

"Jack Daniel's on the rocks," Burbank ordered.

The bartender exchanged a significant glance with a man sitting across the bar from Burbank.

"So as Ah was atellin you," the man said in a wheezy voice to the barkeep, "the broad she started blowin Guy, so Guy he said, 'Look honey, Ah love this but Ah don't eat.' So she said, 'Ah'm not surprised, because last night you tole me you don't like oysters.' Which shows she's a pretty smart broad. She has some broads workin fur her, door to door, introducing a new line of sanitary napkins."

"Well, whut you know," the barkeep said.

Burbank picked up the glass with a shaking hand, intending to sip the drink. But, knowing how painful the first drink could be, he resigned himself and just gulped it, causing the bartender and the man to exchange another deep glance. Burbank remembered Jackson Ward, Richmond's black ghetto. Shack-like houses running down the narrow streets, with their sagging porches, leaky roofs, the broken brick sidewalks pitted, sunken, treacherous. Rooms smelling of smoky kerosene lamps, cockroaches jumping off tables when wicks were turned up, stacks of paper-bagged soft coal, smell of lard in the peeling wallpaper, black kids singing, dancing, imitating their parents having sex. He remembered the lacy, red, hard-fibered stockings with the pungent colored Christmas candy, and the kindergarten smell of paste, and the baby-powder smell of some of the lady teachers, and Bill Maloney who died because an old woman threw a bucket of water on him in winter, causing him to swallow a wad of apple tobacco, which made him get pneumonia, and Fred Epsom the coal man's son with the soft eyes and red hair, who got himself killed by his younger brother when they were fooling with the .22, and the smell of hot dough at night, the look of doughnuts browning in a copper vat, the hiss of gas jets, and the steamroller spewing cinders, and the calliope coming down Broad Street, the sound carrying to Marshall, and watching cockfights in the backyard and smelling chicken droppings in the barn and in the scarifying sun. And he remembered the family of eggs in Jackson Ward. The dad was Billy-egg, the mom Muley-egg, the kids were Micey-egg, Tooty-egg and Loogy-egg. Tooty-egg wore pigtails, her ears were pierced and she was already screwing although she was thirteen. Micey-egg had his mom's ashy black skin and stole from the Broad Street stores. Billy-egg, tall, full-throated, chocolate-skinned, wore a greasy brown stocking cap, sold corn liquor and when he was mad used a bowie knife. Micey-egg and Tooty-egg stuck together like Siamese twins. Micey-egg, rangy, electric, was ready to use a bowie himself.

He recalled the laconic smith with the leather apron, big hands, filthy boots. Lived alone in a room behind the shop. Never mentioned family, friends, outings, past. Burbank had been quick to sense when the old man wanted something out of reach—a pair of tongs, a piece of leather, an iron chunk— and would get it for him. The smith had his eye on him, knowing Burbank had a smith's body, a wrestler's build, solid, chunky, lasting forever. Burbank remembered the glowing coals, the searing cinder smell, the June bugs in the cobbled yard. And inside, the dark, the gloom, thick with iron dust, floor earthen, shoes lying around, iron pigs, the pounding of softened candy-orange metal against the anvil, a horse against the slats, steaming, leg raised, nostrils working, head turned to observe the squatting man. This was in a neighborhood that had rotted away. Only the cobbled street with its gleaming stones and the manure dry and gold-yellow was as good as new.

"Who's Shorty?" he asked the bartender.

"Well, hit ain't *me*," the man replied.

"Why, how tall are you?" Burbank asked.

"Tall enough," the man said.

"You don't look all that tall to *me*," Burbank said.

"Mr. Burbank, Ah don't want any trouble," the barkeep said.

"So you know who I am."

"Everybody aroun here knows about you."

"Knows *what* about me?" Burbank demanded.

"Ain't it obvious?"

"Then what do you know about my *Emperor? Is* the shaft busted or not?"

"Not for me to say."

"What you people have down here? Maybe the FBI or the CIA ought to have a look into what's going on down here! The word gets around mighty fast, I see. What's your name?"

"Slim," the man replied, then laughed, to Burbank's surprise, revealing badly decayed teeth. "See whut Ah'm standin on? Hit's below floor level. *Shorty!*"

"You been bartending all your adult life?" Burbank asked.

"Hell no," Slim grunted. "Ah was a *de*tective in D.C."

"Slim, tell Mr. Burbank how you killed the two guys in D.C.," the man sitting across the bar from Burbank said in his wheezy voice.

"See, suh," Slim began earnestly, staring into Burbank's eyes with a boldness that startled Burbank, "a number of liquor stores they been held up on Saturdays. We decide it's the work of the same two guys. So we stake out some of our guys in liquor stores every Saturday. Ah'm staked out in back of a store. Mah buddy he has hissef a load on. Hit makes me jumpy, when Ah'm on a job Ah like to know Ah kin depend on mah buddy. There's no parteeshun in this little store, so Ah make me one out of some cartons. Mah buddy he takes hissef a nap. I tell the clerk that if the holdup men come in he say, 'Whut! Not *agin!*' as a signal. Cause they might ask for the dough in whispers or gestures, like this, you see? Ah'm readin a magazine when Ah hear the signal. Ah drop it. One of the men he see it an come to the back of the store to see whut's goin on. He has his gun on me afore Ah'm ready. Mah buddy he wake up an make a noise as he shoves his chair. So Ah reach, point the gun at the guy like *this*."

The bartender, looking triumphant, cocked his hand and pointed a stubby forefinger at Burbank's head.

"POW!" the barkeep cried, startling Burbank. "Ah *knew* he was a goner. The bullet it hits in the side of the head an comes out his eye. Mah buddy he fires five or six rounds at the second guy even though Ah'm in the line of fire. Ah duck to keep from being hit. We had tole the clerk to drop if we got action. He did. We run outside. The second guy, he turns an fires a shot at me an misses. Ah point the gun at him like *this*. POW! The bullet it hits him in the chest. He dies on the sidewalk bout twenty minutes later."

There was a long silence.

"Fill her up," Burbank ordered.

After a while, still on the stool, Burbank napped. He dreamed he and Ethel were walking along the edge of a man-made cliff outside Damascus. A great subway had been dug on their left. There was a lot of loose earth down there. Syrians were sitting on the cliff edge, observing an immense, tube-like structure up ahead that rested at right angles to the subway, blocking it. The structure apparently was an experimental jet but it looked too clumsy for flight. Tractors separated it into two sections. Then Burbank saw it was a mockup made of dried gray mud. Some Syrians drew close to him. Were they circus performers? Standing beside a seated woman, a tall Syrian man massaged her shoulders. She was pretty, young, sturdily built. Her shoulders were caked with gray dirt and her breasts were so dirty with it Burbank couldn't make out the nipples. Her belly was dark-skinned, firm. Then he saw with astonishment that her dark vulva was flagrantly exposed. Because it had been shaved, it was a fine gray from the stubble. So although she was a woman, her vulva looked like a child's and was open in a remarkably candid way. The opening resembled Edison's electric bulb, pear-shaped, with a filament down the middle. Burbank's right hand, idly playing in some loose dirt (he and Ethel were seated), felt a coin that he was sure was ancient, maybe from the time of Saint Paul. The Syrians would confiscate it if he made its discovery known. The Syrian stopped massaging the woman. He stared at Burbank. Would the Syrians catch him, Burbank, breaking their law and put him through a secret trial? "Who *are* you?" the woman suddenly demanded very rudely. She didn't seem naked any longer, or covered with dirt. She looked capable, a pioneer spirit, and acutely political. "An American citizen, a bank president!" he replied loudly, almost joyously, knowing that his identity was beyond question. Looking surprised, she studied him carefully. He would have liked to say something in Arabic but he knew that if he tried to he would weaken his position. "I don't believe it," she said finally, smiling maliciously, and she consulted in whispers with the man. "*What* don't you believe?" Burbank asked. "That you're an American citizen, a bank president," she said, glaring. "How many rubles are there to a dollar?" he demanded, bringing into the open and forcefully the obvious Russian connection. She didn't seem to understand. She consulted with the man again. "Never

mind," Burbank said loudly, "I'll bet you a hundred thousand."
"A hundred thousand?" she asked, startled. "*Four* hundred
thousand! A million!" he shouted. The man and woman consulted in whispers. The man said sternly, "Return to your
hotel and remain there until we call for you. Your wife will
stay here." Burbank surreptitiously slipped the coin into his
trouser cuff. He rose and returned to the hotel. But at the
hotel he realized it was twenty to twelve! On the stroke of
noon Ethel had to have her digitalis or she would die! It was
here in the room! Why had he left her so casually, without
explaining to the man, the crowd? And why hadn't she complained? It would take too long to rush the digitalis to her!
Besides, he was forbidden to leave the hotel! He had killed
her! His heart pounded.

Waking up, he thought, "Thank God I didn't kill her!"

Depriving her of her digitalis! He felt awful about it. Partly
the feeling was the result of the drink. Drinking often did that
to him, made him feel he was letting somebody down.

He paid the bartender and took up his former place on the
highway shoulder. But he had no better luck this time than
before. How was he going to make it back to poor Ethel? And
to Nuncle, whom he suddenly had a great longing to see, that
peppery-tempered, indomitable, brilliant little bird? One
morning at the Hilton in Cairo, in their suite that overlooked
the filthy Nile, which didn't have any of the charm of the
James, the Chickahominy (decent Virginia streams), drying
her face, whose color sometimes suggested jaundice, Ethel had
grinned happily at him, showing her even little teeth and
sunken eyes, and had said, "Papa Duck, isn't Egypt *exciting?*"
in her tremulous, musical voice, her head probably roaring
with sentences from Holy Writ. At times in that Holy Land
heat she had a misty, cloudy, far-off look, and he imagined
her heart going full tilt, the valve straining, skipping. He re-

membered now a young woman pumping milk from her breast into a glass bottle, and a baby with a cleft lip like a terrible sword gash, crying in her mother's arms. In Cairo the Burbanks had visited the Coptic Church of St. Sergius in the old part of town and seen the crypt under the church. A damp vaulted chapel with Roman marble columns. It had been flooded often by the Nile's rising. The church guide, stout, wearing a soiled tieless white shirt and limp dark trousers, said in his soft, husky, high-pitched voice that the Holy Family had spent some time in it during their flight to escape Herod's wrath. As they were leaving the church, Burbank noticed Ethel dabbing at her eyes with a handkerchief. "It's terrible how Herod slaughtered them," she said. "Slaughtered who?" "The children." "What children?" "Of Bethlehem." "That what you're crying about?" "No. Mary." "Mary who?" "The Virgin." "Oh," he said. In the Omayad Mosque in Damascus they were shown a large wooden structure, dome-covered, gilded, surmounted by a golden crescent. This was the tomb that contained the head of John the Baptist, their guide said. Ethel cried, "Oh that poor man! To think they cut off his head and it's here! He who baptized our dear Lord!" And, bending her head, she wept uncontrollably, causing some nearby workmen to turn to see who was weeping so bitterly.

However, Burbank's luck hadn't run out, for by God if Spineless George, he of the immortal stiff-kneed walk, dead hair, dead eyes, dead teeth, greasy jeans and shoes, didn't show up from behind a wall of the Edward Garage, hoist his frame onto a motorcycle that until now had managed to escape Burbank's notice, drive it across the highway with an unbelievable roar that reverberated in the open landscape as if it were hammering with insane speed back and forth in a narrow canyon, and pull alongside Burbank. But Burbank, old, proven foe that he was, knew all too well the meaning of that roar. It was designed to put him out of countenance on this Day after Thanksgiving, reminding him as it did of the roar his Emperor once had but didn't have yesterday afternoon nor yesterday evening nor last night nor this morning nor now, and might not have tomorrow. The future, though, including Mist Edward's, Jud James's and most certainly Spineless George's, was still obscure, and Burbank wasn't about to bet he was on the losing side this early in the game. He was well used to savage roars in the jungle world of banking, so dim-witted Spineless George was wasting his noise.

"Don't you all worry none, suh. *Ah* kin git you where you need to go. Least mah ole Harley kin," Spineless George said in a gentle, sympathetic, worried, almost tender voice.

"What's it going to cost me?" Burbank asked.

Spineless George looked startled, maybe shocked.

"Why, Ah jist tryin to be a good Samaritan, Mr. Burbank."

"What *for?*" demanded Burbank suspiciously.

"Suh?" Spineless George said softly, bewildered.

"What's it going to *cost* me?" Burbank still wanted to know.

"Nothin!" said Spineless George angrily, startling Burbank. "Nothin! Nothin! Nothin!"

The word seemed to have stuck in his throat.

"Ah jist want to hep you," he said, but this time so softly that for a second Burbank failed to catch his drift. Again he surprised Burbank by the sudden shift in decibels. Burbank had to admit to himself that this Spineless George was a little beyond him.

"All right," he relented, "but I'm going to have a look first."

And he proceeded to inspect the machine carefully, as if to check it out for possible violations of the motor vehicle code. What he saw gave him something to think about. The bike was a huge, long, heavy thing whose extensive and brilliant chrome work dazzled even his Emperor-accustomed eyes. Its four fat exhaust pipes were chromed, as were its heavy springs, backrest and many other items besides. The bike forced Burbank to reconsider his original estimate of its owner, with whom he now sensed he had an elusive but nonetheless vital kinship, albeit one not of his own choosing.

"What's your sign?" Spineless George asked suddenly.

"Capricorn!" Burbank shot back.

"*Ah* know how it feels to be in trouble. That's why Ah come out here after peekin through some slats an seein how you were gittin nowhere. Heck, hit'll *git* you there!"

"Get me *where?*" demanded Burbank.

"Ah'm jist a daddyless boy. Ah don't know when Ah was *born*, suh, bein a bastard an all."

"You sure you're a bastard?"

"Mah ole lady she tole me long ago. She never *could* say who mah *real* daddy was. Dad! Daddy! Come here, mah boy! Oh mah true son! Oh Lord, whut Ah done that's so terrible you gotta punish me so?"

"Quit that! There's room for all, including a bastard or two," Burbank said sternly.

"Ah thank my stars Ah got Mist Edward, cause whut would Ah do if Ah didn't have *him?* But sometimes Ah'd like to *kill* him, you know? Comes over me like an itch when he's abendin over, back turned to me, me holdin a monkey wrench, an oney him an me in the garage. WHUM! DONE!"

"Cut that out!" Burbank ordered loudly, staring fiercely into Spineless George's eyes. "You ought to get down on your knees in front of that man! He's your *employer*, and don't you forget it! I'm a Capricorn," he added as though to reassure himself. "You going to give me a lift or not?"

"You *bet*, suh!"

Burbank joined Spineless George on the bike.

"It'd be best if you was to hug me real tight, this road bein under repair," Spineless George said.

They took off, and the Harley settled down to a steady, almost gentle humm-purr. As soon as they reached the Thunderbird, Spineless George drove off back toward Yazoo. Then who should run up to Burbank but Mr. Philip Johnston, restaurant manager and ex parte communicant.

"I see you got a lift," Johnston commented.

"Were you *spying* on me?" Burbank asked, setting his jaw.

"Why *gracious* no!" said Johnston a bit breathlessly. "Ossie, your waitress last night, finds you *very* attractive. I heard her tell the chef, and boldly too, that you turn her on. Now isn't that marvelous, considering your age? I hope that when I'm your age I'll have *half* your charisma. Men live and fall by their cars, and women, especially young ones, are turned on by great cars."

"So what's the outlook for my Emperor? I'm sure there are plenty of rumors floating around."

"To be frank, the prognosis isn't good. If I were you I'd brace myself. Then, if things turn out bad, you'll have already tasted the worst. Is something the matter? You look so strange. Are you all right?"

"I'm fine," Burbank said in a tired, trembling voice and reached into his pocket and took a swig of the breath sweetener.

"Sir, I want to offer you my car," Johnston said. "Not that you'd condescend to use it under ordinary circumstances, but these aren't ordinary ones, as you know. There are holes in the floorboards but you have little choice, it seems to me, respectfully speaking. The engine, however, *purrs*. Won't you borrow it for the duration?"

"Duration of *what?*"

"As long as you care to stay in these parts. This isn't lift country, Mr. Burbank. About Mrs. Burbank's parcel, the rule wasn't meant for you and yours but for common farm folk, ordinary people."

"Don't you know we're a democracy?" asked Burbank sternly. "Well don't ever forget it!"

And he crossed the asphalt driveway that lay between the restaurant and the motel, leaving Johnston to contemplate his departing stocky figure. Then he turned around and, walking slowly back to Johnston, at whom he stared, asked, "Well, where is it?"

Johnston, electrified (or so it appeared), led him to an area-way behind the restaurant, where he introduced him to a beat-up, dusty, ivory Chevy two-door sedan.

"What are you doing with Delaware plates?" Burbank asked suspiciously.

"I've been here only eight months. It's perfectly legal. Calm yourself. Everything's in order."

"What will it cost me?"

"*Nothing*. It will be my pleasure and honor, sir."

"Hm," Burbank said, and slipped behind the wheel. The engine turned over, coughed, caught hold. "You said it *purrs!*" he exclaimed, looking accusingly at Johnston. "Why do you *exaggerate?* Facts, damn it, are the only thing that'll save you people. Can't you get that through your skulls? Your whole structure is nothing but froth."

He got out of the car.

"Will you accept?" Johnston asked.

"No," Burbank replied dryly.

"Sir, that hurts. After all, it *goes*."

"Is that a slur on my Emperor?"

"Gracious, I only mean it'll *get* you there."

"Get me *where? Where* are you people trying to *get* me?" Burbank demanded, standing stockily, powerfully, and looking up at Johnston's sallow, almost ashen face. "You got it wired to explode? *That* it?"

"Good Lord!" Johnston breathed.

Upon which Burbank stared at him a moment, then abruptly crossed the highway to the nameless garage, which was in a different, milky light now from the afternoon light of yesterday. And the vast sky looked and felt damper than before. Hearing voices, he went around to the back. The two men of yesterday were leaning against the wooden garage wall, facing the sun and eating sandwiches of white bread smeared with strong-smelling peanut butter. There was something about the way they appraised him that led him to think they had expected him.

"Bad bearin," John Carradine said.

"Bad shaft too, Profit, Ah'll bet," the first man said.

"Bad *shaft?*" Burbank asked loudly, feeling his heart pumping. "Bad *shaft*, you say? Is there a car around here I can rent?"

"Heck, Ah'll rent you mah Raleigh," John Carradine said with a chuckle.

"Where is it?" Burbank asked quickly.

"Over there," John Carradine replied, pointing a long, bony finger.

The finger, and indeed the hand, trembled, and Burbank remembered George Forman. Turning, he saw a three-speed bicycle that would have made a bike lover break down and cry, it was so down on its luck. He went up to it. The wheels were rusty, the chain was begging for grease. Burbank felt the tires. They were as soft as mush. He shivered, glanced around at the weather and remembered a dream he had had (last night? the night before?).

He was visiting old George, and George was a doctor friend. But no, he, Burbank, was an apprentice of George's, and George was a dentist without a license. However, it was okay, he wasn't going to treat anybody's teeth, he was only going to pretend to treat them. But a guy came into the office, looking severe, and asked, "You got any four-by-five papers?" Burbank said "No," so the guy left. Burbank, wearing a tight white cotton jacket like an apron, moved about the office in a soft-shoe strut, glancing around until he was satisfied there were no four-by-five papers in it. Another guy came in, looking officious, and asked, "Did you get fours and fives in your tests?" Burbank said "Yes," not knowing what the guy meant. "Let me see them," the guy said with the tone of somebody em-powered to investigate phony dentists. Fearful, Burbank glanced around for help. Then he saw that old George had disappeared and that he, Burbank, was alone with the official. "I don't have them with me," he muttered lamely. The official looked ferocious. Burbank gathered it was a crime not to have them with him at all times. He said helplessly, "I haven't been myself lately." Then the official turned out to be Jeb, Burbank's son, but he went off aggressively nonetheless, possibly to sum-mon the police. Then Burbank realized he was staying in a motel with some guy. The room was a mess, beds crumpled, bedding rolled. The guy was showering. Burbank proceeded to shave. The hair on the right side of his head was too long, it came down over his ear. Shaving his sideburn, he chopped off some of the head hair by mistake. Whole parts of his face resisted the razor blade. Ethel came in for something. They spoke vaguely to each other. Then she took one of his white shirts that was still fresh from the laundry and dropped it into the wet basin. *Well* now! This irritated him just a little! How-ever, he kept his temper because he was furiously coping with the left side of his face, feeling for stubble and scraping away, over and over. The blade wasn't cutting worth a damn. He looked closely at the tube and what did it say but Nivea! He was angry with her for having set her Nivea down among his things! He turned to shout at her but she had vanished. Then the guy came in and it was Jeb! Upon which Burbank awoke, furious with both Jeb and Ethel.

He recalled the time he had spent with George in Mexico not so long ago (but not long ago depended on who was keeping time). They had had three days of fishing off Acapulco with rotten luck and had quit and gone up to Mexico City, where George had an apartment, leaving the wives in Acapulco. It was a penthouse apartment with a maid, an afghan hound and lots of pre-Columbian sculpture. It overlooked a park. George had inherited a powerful income, a sense of humor and great health. He had become a vegetarian sometime back, loved nuts, dates, carrot juice, nut waffles with gobs of whipped cream. They drove down to Cuernavaca, where George ran into some people he knew, an Italian from L.A. (formerly from the Lake Maggiore district, also seven years in Buenos Aires), a priest, and a blind Cuban with a daughter, a white cane and dark glasses. The Cuban, a small, lean, dark guy, almost gaunt, and with cold hands like claws, would glance up at George with a sudden glitter of glasses. He spoke loudly but his daughter, who wasn't pretty, was silent. The priest, a guy who loved his wine, had been traveling around the country. The Italian had a brilliant smile. The Cuban bought a straw basket from a spastic old Indian sitting on small cobblestones, surrounded by odors of maize, tacos, grease, smoke, manure. The Cuban's hands felt the wares expertly. The Indian, helpless, seemed to shiver. In the evening George and Burbank were in a bar, and a big young American was sitting with a small foreign-looking guy, and the big guy tried to break the little guy's thumb but the little guy was slippery, so the big guy tried to break George's thumb but George slipped his hand free, and the big guy glared at old George. The big guy said, "I can take you over, I'm an FBI agent." "Are you now," George

said. The big guy grunted and hit George's arm. The angry
bartender said to the big guy, "Please, you stop fighting here."
The big guy hit George hard in the shoulder. George said,
"Listen, you phony," grabbed him by the collar and slammed
him in the face, knocking him down. When the big guy got
up, mouth bleeding, he avoided looking at George. He and
the little guy left. Next day George and Burbank were at a
novillada in Mexico City at a place called Rancho del Charro,
and George hated to think those three young bulls would be
asked to fight, they were so thin, afraid, they had to be chased,
cornered. A tall, brown-haired American, who looked as if he
lived on stilts, chased the first one around the ring, crying
"Miró!" When he stuck the bands in, the bull twisted his neck
in an effort to get rid of them, stuck out his long pointed tongue
and drooled and bawled. George stood up and shouted, "Let
him go!" and Burbank could see the American bullfighter
flinch. The bull stumbled, fell, had to be helped to his feet.
He kept running around the ring, looking to escape. George
stood up again and shouted, "Let him *go*, you son of a bitch!"
No passes were possible. A couple of Mexicans in dirty uni-
forms, one with patches in the seat of his pants, killed the bull.
The ring, which was only half a ring, smelled of dust, smoke,
barns. Men in a nearby house were nailing boards.

And now old George . . . the hurt birds.

Burbank returned to the motel and entered the office. The
motel manager appeared from a back room, making his way
forward with a strange, tortuous weaving of hips (or was it a
mincing of steps?), and took up his place behind the red counter
with the little chrome bell. Well who should it be but Mr.
Philip Johnston himself! Which gave Burbank a start!

"You the manager here *too?*" Burbank asked.

"*Yes* sir," said Johnston softly, with a smile.

"Why didn't you *tell* me? Why are you people so *sneaky?*"

Burbank exploded, determined to come to grips with some-thing.

Johnston threw his head back and laughed, causing Burbank to laugh also while at the same time noticing that Johnston's neck was scrawnier than he had taken it to be, with a sur-prisingly large Adam's apple and with tufts of hair growing at the base as if Johnston was afraid to shave there.

"Mr. Burbank," Johnston said slowly, and there was no trace of a laugh or even of a smile on his countenance now, "my sole desire is to be of some service to you, however small. Why else would I offer you my Chevy, when surely you understand how ashamed I am of it? My Chevy represents my life-style just as clearly as your Emperor does yours. The floorboards of my life, sir, have been worn through. That Chevy was raised from the dead, it was in a terrible crash before I got it, and it's had so many transfusions it's a miracle it's still alive. Still, it runs, and that's something. Not that I mean to hint at the condition of your Emperor. It's very plain to see that you're a mover and shaker, sir, but my Chevy can be of some service to you nevertheless."

"You were spying on me! Where were you standing?"

"Why, in the kitchen," Johnston said, waving toward the room from which he had emerged.

"Who put you up to it?"

"I stand there often, looking at the passing parade, wishing it was me and mine that was going to Miami and the Keys. But how far would my Chevy get? My mother always used to say, 'Be prepared for an accident at all times, Philly, wear clean underwear.' Now take you, sir, and your great Emperor, where's the embarrassment in breaking down in a great car like that? And even if my Chevy didn't break down, how'd I get my whole family into it?"

"What do you do in the kitchen? Hit the sauce, that your problem? You the cook too?"

"I don't know a thing about cooking."

"But you know a lot about spying."

"Gracious," said Johnston, "I thought we were friends."

"You want to sell me your Chevy, that it? At an exorbitant profit? Why not? We're all out for dough and number one."

"Listen, Mr. Burbank, you know how many kids I've got? Eleven. The Church says only celibacy or the rhythm method will do. I've tried celibacy for half a year at a time but it makes for terrible fights. My wife's period is very irregular, so the rhythm method lets us down."

Burbank asked, "What's this got to do with me? You manage the garage over there too? No? Who does?"

"Why, nobody. It's so small it manages itself."

And Johnston laughed heartily again, once again causing Burbank to join in. Not that there was much to laugh about from Burbank's point of view.

"Who owns it then?" Burbank asked.

"Mist Edward, of course."

"MIST EDWARD?" Burbank shouted the words, for the name, coming at this juncture, electrified him. "Why didn't you *tell* me? Why are you always trying to surprise me around here? And how come he has those butcher hands, so red and meaty?"

"He used to work in a slaughterhouse in Baltimore and he still goes there now and then, moonlighting."

"Doing *what?*"

"Cutting throats, of course."

Burbank abruptly left the office.

"Mr. Burbank!" Johnston called after him excitedly, but Burbank had turned off his hearing aid, figuratively speaking.

He hadn't gone far on his way to the motel proper, with its

long arcade, when he heard a "Pss!" His back stiffened as he turned to observe a small wiry woman approach him.

"I'm Jody Johnston, Mr. Burbank. I overheard what Phil told you in there," she said in a deep, trembling voice. "What can I do? I'm not trying to smother him. I'm only being *me*, the girl he married. Oh Mr. Burbank, will you please help me?"

"*Help* you! Who do you think I *am?*" he said. "I'm just a banker, passing through. My business is money—the dirty stuff that makes this nation spin. Who do you take me for? You think I'd be here this minute if my Emperor wasn't on the blink? I'd be *whish*, down in Carolina by now. You think I get along with my wife? I hit the hoochinoo because of her, I get dried out at very expensive joints. Go see your priest, bishop, Pope. That's what they're there for, isn't it? Don't they know all about women from firsthand experience?"

There was a silence, during which her brown eyes, large and expressive, studied him intently. Then she turned her back on him and walked toward the office, her hips broad, stiff, disjointed-looking.

FEELING HE NEEDED A WALK BADLY TO CLEAR his head, Burbank went to the end of the motel grounds and crossed a field. To his surprise, the field was a rich green, and its bristling grass looked as if it had been sprinkled with a glistening powder. He heard a rooster crowing nearby and recalled how he was awakened at around four in the morning by a rooster near his window who crowed his brains out for a couple of hours. This was in Jerusalem, City of Peace, crowded on its hilly plateau, surrounded on three sides by valleys filled with the battle debris of millennia. Ethel's breathing had been shallow but regular. How many nights had he lain and listened away from home with her, afraid her breathing might stop after a seizure!

The Eastern Shore rooster crowed again, stridently, as if his throat was made of metal. Burbank imagined the rooster stretching on his claws, gazing fiercely out of garnet eyes and swelling until his face feathers quivered. On the Via Dolorosa, following the Stations of the Cross, the Burbanks had visited the Church of the Holy Sepulcher, where Ethel looked so taut and peaked he was afraid she'd keel over. And she was ashen in the Church of the Nativity in Bethlehem, where even his own heart thumped because of the heat and the close air. What a glare when they stepped into the church's courtyard! The ivory-colored stones of the floor and walls lunged at them like fangs. Next day the Burbanks drove to the Jordan, which was little more than a slick desert stream, a fast-running creek. Thickets of willow, poplar and tamarisk lined the banks. In the east were phosphorescent hills and beyond them faint, trembling amber ones. Turning, Burbank saw Ethel wading across the river. She had slipped off her dress and gone in, wearing a green bathing suit. The only obvious sign of her heart condition was in her legs, which tended to get heavy with water. He observed her in silence. You had to respect a woman who took the Jordan seriously. She filled a little bottle with holy water and when she reached the bank she handed it to him for safekeeping. He recognized it as an heirloom from her grandmother: crystal with a sterling screwtop.

He remembered naked Strawberry Hill overlooking smaller wooded hills, and down in the woods was a wide crick, brush running to the water's edge, weeping-willow strands hanging over it, the water muddy, warm, with leaves, webs, orange dust and waterskates, smelling dusty, tasting earthy, the shore slimy, and from the top of the hill you saw the country round about. Terrible Union charges had been repulsed here. And the night was moonless, and mosquitoes buzzed incessantly, coming from the swampy hollows where you came on rusted bits of camp and trench life: whitened fat bullets, metal buttons, cannonballs, broken pots, bottle slivers. He recalled seeing in the Confederate Museum brown linen havelocks, woolen headwarmers, redware canteens like large thin doughnuts, sharpshooter rifles made by rural gunsmiths, the sword Lee wore at Appomattox, the pen he signed the surrender terms with, Stonewall Jackson's sword, and things made by Confederate soldiers in Union prisons: a wooden chain, a necklace of gutta-percha buttons, a hair chain made of horse tails. And upstairs Jeff Davis's doeskin gloves, hard collar, paper cutter, engraved Colt Navy revolver. And the small, neat garden, smelling of honeysuckle and English boxwood, where Jeff Davis's little boy had died in a fall from the balcony. As for Grant and Lincoln, Mama Duck had inherited some large oval prints in gold frames of famous Americans and brought them out of storage, where they had been for years, and hung them in the dining room of the Princeton house dominated by the great mahogany table Burbank had had made in Guatemala, and he had taken these gents and stuck them in the basement with their faces to the wall.

The Eastern Shore road meandered past beatup frame houses with smoking chimneys, sagging porches, chicken coops, jalopies, old tires, stacked cordwood, then descended to a trough flanked by scrub pine. Here Burbank's nerves were jolted by the honking of a horn, and a car stopped beside him. It contained one person, the waitress of yesterday.

"Quit tooting at me," he said dryly.

"I was only being friendly," she retorted. "It was my friend's idea. I said, 'No, he won't appreciate it.' Maria said, 'I'm sure he'll like it.' I said, 'I've met him. I know him. A tough customer.' She said, 'You mean that charming Mr. Burbank with those fine little feet? He's tenderhearted underneath. Be friendly to him.' I said, 'You don't know him.' She said, 'Because I didn't have a formal introduction? Didn't I watch him from the kitchen like a mother?' "

"Whut was she doing in the *kitchen?*" he asked, feeling alarmed for some reason.

There was a pause. Her dark hair was curly. Her nose was long and looked as if it had been broken. It caused her to speak nasally. Her chin was bold. Her eyes were larger than they had looked yesterday and not as almond-shaped as he had thought. She had a little smile that she produced by pulling down the corners of her mouth while revealing horse teeth.

"She's a dishwasher and general helper," she said.

"She also *cook?*" he asked suspiciously.

"Only when the chef wants a Greek flavor."

"Greek flavor hell," he retorted.

She opened large eyes.

"Was she *spying* on me?" he demanded.

"No, don't put it like that. Just because she works in the kitchen is no reason to accuse her of things. It's slop, slop, work, work, vapors, clouds, garbage, flames from burning steaks, smell of gas and onions, lard frying, chitlins cooking, dough, sweet marjoram."

"You married?" he asked suddenly.

"Why? What's so great about marriage?"

She lowered her head with an odd little gesture, as if in resignation.

"What happened?" he asked.

"I went with Luke. *You* know Luke. I had problems but he knew about them. His doctor friend, Mylum, told him, 'If you marry her don't have kids. She's mentally bereft.' As you know, Luke's a lot older than me. He had fatherly feelings toward me. So we got married, and then after a while I wanted a baby. So I kept after him about it. I'd say, 'I *need* one. *Yours.* I feel useless without one. I'll start fooling around if you don't give me one.' So he thought it over and decided to risk it. When I came home from the hospital I refused to go near the baby. Whenever I got close to her I started to gasp, my chest felt smashed, I got dizzy, I was afraid I'd faint and fall on her. Luke kept saying, 'Why don't you go to your own flesh and blood? What's the *matter* with you?' So I said, 'Well, you *know* I'm mentally bereft.' He'd say, 'You begged and begged to have a baby and now you won't go near it! What are we going to *do?*' I said, 'Let's give her out for adoption.' His eyes popped. '*Adoption?* That's my flesh and blood! I don't knock off a kid just to give it away! I'll kill you first, you maniac! You're destroying me, you nut-hound!' It drives me crazy when people are careless with words, so I shouted, 'I may be mentally bereft but I'm not a *nut-hound—because there's no such word!* How *dare* you abuse me, knowing I'm mentally bereft!' '*Abuse you?*' he shouted, waving his arms. 'I'll send you to a *nut-hatch!* I should have sent you to a nut-hatch long ago!' "

"What's this got to do with *me?*" Burbank demanded loudly in an agitated voice.

"Don't interrupt! You'll see in a minute! I could stand anything, but I couldn't stand his using words that *didn't exist*. I screamed, 'You say nut-hatch once more and I'll kill that baby! I swear it by my mom's life! I will *not* have you talk to me with words that *don't exist!*' So he said softly, 'Don't harm that innocent baby, Ossie. That little baby never did you any harm. I'll never say it again. I thought it was a real word. Honest to God I did.' But I still couldn't go near her, so we had to hire a nurse. He looked dazed, bewildered. The more dazed he looked the more I picked on him. I'd say, 'Where you been? You're fifteen minutes late. You've been with a woman, you mother, I can smell her perfume.' He'd say, 'Be reasonable, what could I do with a woman in fifteen minutes? This is soap you're smelling.' So I'd shout, 'Stop quibbling!' I'd search his clothes, wallet, papers. I'd wake up in the middle of the night and a voice would say, 'Evidence! Find the evidence!' So he developed headaches, earaches, back trouble, and he saw Mylum, and Mylum said, 'Look, I *told* you there's nothing wrong with you, your trouble is in your environment.' So Luke got angry and said, 'What do you mean, environment? You mean Ossie, right? You know she's mentally bereft!' So Mylum said, 'What do you *expect* me to say? Dump your loving wife, Ossie?' So Luke would come home exhausted, tell me everything and start to cry. Meanwhile I smoked in bed a lot, and I burned a blanket, then a pillow, then my fingers, and Luke was afraid I'd burn the house down. And I wouldn't let him touch me. When he tried to touch me—"

"Why are you telling me all this?" Burbank shouted suddenly in an agitated voice, and crossed the road and walked rapidly back toward the Thunderbird.

"Wait! I haven't finished!" she cried.

She started the engine and caught up with him.

"So whose side are you on, mine or Luke Edward's?" she cried.

Burbank stopped in his tracks and stared at her as if for the first time.

"Luke Edward?" he asked uneasily. "He any relation to Mist Edward?"

"*Why* are you teasing me? He *is* Mist Edward and you *know* it! Why do you think I bothered to *tell* you all this!" she cried, and she drove off angrily in a burst of exhaust.

Reaching the motel, Burbank entered the restaurant, where lunch was being served, caught sight of Philip Johnston, walked up to him and said in an uncertain, agitated voice, "Your Chevy still available?"

"You just *bet!*" Johnston cried, observing his face carefully. "Through the door," he said, pointing.

Spotting the Chevy on the other side of the areaway, Burbank strode over to it and got in. Johnston handed him the key. Without another word Burbank swung onto the highway. The back of the Chevy seemed only vaguely connected with the front. Gray wornout fields to east and west, land verging on ocean, continents adrift, and he driving to a place called Yazoo to see about the condition of his Emperor. He remembered the Marshall Street bakery in Richmond and the baker's long white creamy neck. The baker got pneumonia and ran naked into the winter night street. They found him a couple of hours later, sitting quietly on a curbstone, enjoying the fresh air. He died the next afternoon.

He remembered the teacher in Richmond who when she stood against his desk pressed her groin against a corner and all the boys talked about her. Once he didn't take his hand away in time and she pressed against his knuckles. *Hinky Dinky Parlez-vous. Yes, We Have No Bananas. Limehouse Blues. Three O'clock in the Morning. Hiawatha. Marcheta. Sweet Genevieve.* The days may come, the day-hays may go. Clang of the firehouse bell. Metallic icewater in the firehouse jug. Milk bottle bigger than a house. Mr. Duffy saying "Let's you two fight," so the guys called him "Let's You Two Fight Duffy."

He remembered the corner of St. James and Jackson in Jackson Ward long, long ago. A summer night. The itinerant black preacher arriving with two middle-aged black ladies in long black skirts; removing his black jacket; speaking in a calm bass voice. People sitting on porches, curbs, crying "Amen!" and "Thass right!" and clapping rhythmically. The preacher working himself up, flailing long arms, leaning far back, far forward, sweating so hard he was soaked through, his head spraying the area with sweat. Lifting his right arm high, swinging it past his toes, crying "Rrr-*ruh!*" in a snarling way. "Now Moses rrr-*ruh!* he been found in the bulrushes rrr-*ruh!* bah the

Pharaoh's daughter rrr-*ruh!* when she come to the river rrr-*ruh!* to wash hersef rrr-*ruh!* An she raise him rrr-*ruh!* like her own son rrr-*ruh!* An he grow strong rrr-*ruh!* An God he say unto him rrr-*ruh!* Ah am that Ah am' rrr-*ruh!*" A listener sobbing. "Lord, why you take mah woman away?" This was Sol Brown, whose wife Ada had recently died in childbirth. A mouse of a woman, she had built a tiny, musty, dim, lard-smelling nest with lots of stuffed furniture. He was chunky, chesty, full of grins. He called each of his male friends "Garbage" and threw parties that were sometimes raided by the cops. The guests would jump out the back windows into the yard below, onto weeds among ailanthus trees.

He remembered a young guy wandering around Princeton: bluish face, deep-blue lips, bluish teeth, hungry body; swaggering in rundown shoes and a yellow Afrikaner straw hat whose brim trembled faintly; a cigarette dripping from his mouth. Also the bright-yellow complexion of a Princeton woman. Sunken eyes with dark glinting eyeballs. Spindle arms. Bone-dry legs. He had seen her eating a sandwich on Nassau Street, wolfing with clawlike fingers. Musculature of jaws operating thin, wiry, powerful mandibles. Also the sight of Magnus Appelbaum (on Fifth Avenue), who had worked in the foreign department and whom Burbank had fired for incompetence. Bristling hairs issuing like black grass out of capacious nostrils. Appelbaum had choked trying to contain tears, made several vague mysterious signs as if writing in the air with his left hand, clutched Burbank's jacket sleeve with buttery moist fingers. His large womanish hand, still (on Fifth Avenue) well knuckled, well fed, bore down on the cane, the fingertips moving occasionally: subtle, secret antennae testing which way the wind of fortune was blowing.

Burbank stopped at Shorty's for a couple of drinks, then parked in front of the Edward Garage.

"That's the biggest shaft we *ever* see. *Whut* a shaft!" Jud James said as soon as he saw Burbank enter the place.

Spineless George stopped what he was doing, came close and stared at Burbank's face.

"But hit done *busted!*" James quickly added. "Whut they go an stroke a shaft like *at* fur? Mist Edward say, 'Built it up! Metalized it! Jist to snake a leetle more jism outa it!' "

"*Busted?*" Burbank cried.

They were observing him intensely with frowns of worry now, or so it seemed to him.

"This Left, our Ballimore expert," James was saying.

"How do," Mr. Left said, smiling. "Yes *suh*. Hit's jist a leetle old chip but mah whut trouble it do cause!"

"Can you get a new one?" Burbank asked. "How long will it take?"

"*Well* now." Jud James took a long breath. "Hit's not oney your shaft, hit's your bearins too, an we got to inspect your pistons, don't we, Left? An tomorruh's Saturday, an *no*body aroun here is fixin to work more in half a day to*mor*ruh. An the next day is Sunday, so you kin say ditto to *hit*. On Monday we kin ask Ballimore to ship the shaft an bearins an gaskets an seals an maybe some old pistons, an if they come on *time*, without bein missing like they usually are, then we kin lickity split the whole theng by Wednesday even, figurin on gitting the stuff by Monday after."

"What's *that?*" Burbank asked, pointing to something on the floor near the Emperor, the highlights of which, flickering in the dimness, seemed to be winking at him.

"Why, your shaft," said James, glancing sharply at Burbank's face.

Feeling unsteady in his gait, Burbank went to the garage door and took several deep breaths, the three men watching him. The cement apron on which he stood threatened to start spinning and swirl up at him. Then, turning to face them, he said harshly, "I'm going to get rid of that *thing*," pointing to the Emperor.

"Why, suh, you caint git rid of *hit*," James said, frowning heavily.

"I'm going to buy myself a brand-new one."

"Hit leaves a fella not knowing *whut* to believe," James said sadly.

"Then believe this," Burbank said grimly. "When a person or a thing has *let you down*, get *rid* of it."

"Sometimes they caint hep it."

"Forgiveness is not a concept of value to business," Burbank said. "If a man working for me talks about forgiveness in business I *fire* him. The only parts I hire a man for are backbone and fists. Business is fight, fight, *fight*," he said, still dizzy but feeling a lot better than he had a moment ago.

"Gawd," said James softly. "Ah never see such a case a guts in mah life. Ah kin take the lil *biddy* breakdowns, but *shaft* trouble—"

"That, sir, is tough titty. One must fight or go under. If a man takes hold and wrestles, gets a full nelson on life and twists—like so—life is bound to cry uncle."

"Suh," James said, taking a long breath, "hit's a pleasure to hear you. Hit's like listenin to TV. Ah better tell Mist Edward."

"I'll tell him myself."

"Hep yourself. He's in the office."

"Don't you worry none," said Burbank, making his way to the office door.

He felt himself recovering fast.

Mist Edward was seated behind his little beatup desk, doodling on a pad, dark glasses flashing.

"*Well* now," he said heartily, rising. "Enjoyin your leetle stay, are you? But whut y'all wanna go an git a shaft like at juiced up fur? Cause all your pistons been shortened. Sure! They build up the shaft an cut the pistons down to soup up the ole compression. *Whut* a mess! Cause we kin git oney a *standard* shaft. Hit's hopeless to try an fix your big one. An Emperor pistons is *some*thin to git."

"I'm going to get rid of that car," Burbank said, watching Mist Edward's face closely, but all he could see was the electric bulb dancing on the specs.

"Well, whut you know. Hit's shaft panic is all. Slow down, suh, an it'll pass. You don't wanna git rid of that theng. An, to speak frankly, Ah don't think you *kin*. You git mah drift?"

"Mist Edward, I'm a busy man," Burbank said. "Time to me is a precious commodity. Now, I mean to mosey along down to the Keys. How come James said there isn't a chance of his men working this weekend?"

"Taint oney a question of work, hit's a question of parts. Parts, *parts!*" Mist Edward said irritably. "How kin they work effen they ain't got no parts? Ballimore ain't go stay open jist to suit lil ole *me*."

"Why can't we get a shaft this afternoon?"

"Hit's plum *closin* time, Mr. B. An Ballimore is closed tight as a drum on Saturday. *Don't* you know that?"

"No, and I doubt it."

Mist Edward flashed his glasses at Burbank.

"Doubt all you want, jist call em an see. That Emperor place is almost *never* open. Hit beats me why a man like your good sef will drive an Emperor in the country. An Emperor's fine in the *city*—if you never *leave* the city. Drive a *Chevy* in the country, those fellas are open for business."

"How soon can you get a shaft then?"

"Suh, this is Friday. Big week-*end*. If it wasn't for mah wife Ossie's younger brother—Ah never *did* see a fella so down on his luck. But he had hissef lotsa gals with names like somethin to eat, ginger, pepper, peaches, olive, an a baleful of dirty pictures up in the attic. He tells me everythin, like Ah'm his daddy, gits me to set down with him an a bottle, hunkers on his heels an shows me pictures he sells in summer. You been to Ocean City, you been there this time of year? Ah urge you, suh, to run over an have a look. Ah been there this past Veterans Day an Ah tell *you* Ah'll never forget at sight long's Ah live. Long empty streets, houses boarded up, mounds of drift sand in the gutters, but Ole Glory flyin from aluminum poles, God bless them civic fellas. See, Ah had this itch to be by mahsef, mah pore head sometimes gits to poundin right back here, so up Ah git an study the ocean from a jetty near the Coast Guard tower. An that Yank up in the tower kept awatchin me to see if Ah was fixin to throw a bomb or somethin, Ah guess, an he young enough to be mah son! Mah head was apoundin so, that gray tower look half a mile high. The girders climbed *and* climbed, crisscrossin. These Yanks never let you beat roun in nothin, they run up on you, hands up don't help none, they gonna kill you anyhow, a man go to say 'Ah' they shoot him right in the mouth, they do in on you with a rifle butt, anythin, many good Southern men gone into the graveyard buck naked with nothin on, the Yanks come after you, you ought to been prayin, most of the country throw a Southerner away, but he's still a man. Ever time he do somethin, he don't aim to be adoin it, he jist do it, hit's one of them thengs. So Ah walk on the beach an had this feelin I ought to git on mah knees an kiss the sand in thanks of being an American, but Ah didn't, whut with him still awatchin me. He up there warm, high-powered rifle, ammo, phone, radio, food, somethin hot to drink, *an* somethin to leak in. *Ah* had to take a leak right bad but was afraid to do it on the beach lessen he have it on me for exposin mahsef, so Ah hold it in till Ah most bust. Ah go up to the boardwalk n snake roun the wood buildins, shacks mostly, looking for a place. Some were boarded up, others you could see all the stuff settin there takin dust—pinball machines, jumpin horses, gypsies tellin your fortune. Sometimes Ah'm outa his sight but mostly Ah see him awatchin me, which wasn't a fair shake, that bein mah own country. So Ah keep goin down the beach, thinkin to lose him roun a turn, but caint, he spyin on me like Ah'm a mad dawg. So Ah lef the beach an went into the streets an when Ah come to a corner Ah stan on the curb and let go into the gutter, mah bladder it like to bust. Hit made me feel life ain't worth livin to have to pee into a Southern street like Ah was a criminal. Whut good's Ole Glory on them poles if Ah caint feel like a *man*? Ah could have dropped to mah knees an cried in the middle of the gutter in thanks of bein Southern born, but that Yank he—"

"*Who* do you think you're filibustering?" Burbank suddenly said angrily.

Mist Edward sat down heavily in what seemed to Burbank astonishment, and his restless glasses glittered.

"I know of *no* village or town or city in this nation that permits public *pissing*," Burbank said. "How'd you know there wasn't some young virgin peeking out of one of those houses? That could scar her for life. And you think I care about your brother-in-law, Ossie's brother? You take me for a bleeding heart? What are you trying to hide? I understand you moonlight in that Baltimore slaughterhouse. You people out on another lynching? Is *that* it?"

Mist Edward's head shook slightly, and his dark specs, in their flashing, looked startled again. Removing his glasses with a quick gesture, he revealed eyes the color of pale slate, with a curious ring of milk-blue circling the iris. Burbank was star-tled to see that strange circle.

"Ah was speaking from mah heart," Mist Edward said softly. "*No* suh, you're flesh an blood like me, like Ossie's brother that's down on his luck, like those fellas out there workin on your Emperor to hep you out. You come to us for hep an we *give* it, best we kin. You have *broke down*, suh, that's a fact of life you caint blink at, an it ain't us folks have done it but your own Yank folks with their dude notions. Now you jist slow down a bit, long enough to be human. Ah'm not here jist to fix your Emperor, Ah'm here to say how do an have a leetle chat to improve our understandin. How come you don't dig at? Suh, if Ah was you Ah'd *dig* it."

"Can you get a shaft in Norfolk?"

"No Emperor place."

"Wilmington?"

"*No* suh."

"D.C.?"

"*That* Emperor place don't *never* wanna do business. Most you kin hope fur is a Ballimore shaft."

"Customized?"

"*Come* on, Mr. B, go on down to your fishin an forgit at stuff. We'll git you a standard shaft. Course, a standard *an* standard pistons ain't go give the jism of a stroked shaft an short pistons, so when you come to a standard an *short* pistons your compression is gonna *drop*. That Emperor joint in Bal-limore don't *never* carry pistons. They tell their customers their old pistons don't never go bad, an to prove it they don't stock em, they stock shafts, though, cause everybody *knows* their shafts go bad."

There was a knock at the door. Jud James poked his head into the room and said to Mist Edward, "The pistons is A-okay," then disappeared. It seemed to Burbank that Mist Edward was downcast, maybe even deeply depressed. Without waiting for another exchange he left the office and the garage, determined to gather his wits about him.

Walking through and beyond the village, he came to an auto graveyard. Cars on top of a rise, on the sloping sides and down a hollow, right side up, upside down, on their fronts, tails, sides, bashed in, torn open, rammed. For a car lover like Burbank it was anguish to see them. The gate was open. He walked in. Then he realized he was standing in front of an Emperor! It was still on its feet but its hindquarters had been bashed in by a terrific force on the left rear side. Now this was DEVAS-TATION, this was TRAGEDY! The interior was enough to break a strong man's heart. Crumpled, disfigured, spattered by slivers of glass, and stained by something dark. A thought came to him that made his stout heart flutter. The front end of this red Emperor was undamaged, apparently. Maybe its shaft was intact and could be transplanted into his own Emperor. He strode through the gate and down the road to Yazoo. Mist Edward was standing in front of the garage, his butcher's hands behind him. With him were Jud James, foreman, and Left. Burbank went up to them.

"I discovered an Emperor in the car graveyard," he said. "The back end is smashed up but the front looks okay."

"*Discovered*, you say?" said Mist Edward and laughed. "Suh, you caint dis*cover* whut's well known, now kin you?"

"Why didn't you mention it then?" Burbank demanded.

"*Mention* it!" said Mist Edward, raising his eyebrows in astonishment. "Why, to spare your *feelins!* Whut kinda fish you take me fur? Ah got *feelins!* We're strong on *feelins* down here! *Feelins* is our *specialty!*"

"Never mind my feelings, *my* feelings are as strong as steel!" Burbank said. "Can you put that red shaft into my Emperor?"

"*Course.*"

"Will you do it *now?*"

"*Course!*" Mist Edward muttered and ran to a beatup green pickup truck parked on the street, jumped in and was away before Burbank knew what he was up to. James, Spineless George (who had come out and joined them) and Left ran after him and piled into the back.

Burbank sat down, closed his eyes, rested awhile, then napped. When he awoke he guessed they had headed for the graveyard, so he followed them in Johnston's Chevy.

"How's the shaft?" he asked, looking around.

They pointed to it. There it was, lying in a pool of oil the earth was soaking up.

"Is it okay?"

"Yes *suh,*" Mist Edward said heavily, and he and his cohorts put their tools in the back of the truck, lifted the shaft, the connecting rods and the connecting-rod bearings onto it and drove off. Burbank followed them to the garage.

"She'll be ready by midnight," Mist Edward said.

Burbank heard his engine roar, felt the old G forces in his back, saw these crackers choking in his exhaust.

"Midnight?"

"Why? Won't midnight do you?"

"What's *really* the score?" Burbank asked.

Mist Edward waited a moment, then said in a voice that had dropped in pitch, as if he suddenly felt exhausted, "The score, suh, is that we're four able-bodied men with too much pork in our blood and lard in our liver, but we have not been messed up by a mess of city livin."

"I have your word on midnight?"

"Mah word? Ah say *midnight* an he wants mah *word!* An after Ah been spreadin mahsef to hep him, a stranger in our midst. You want yoursef a contract, that it, Mr. B? Looka here, we eat grits, hush puppies, corn pone, but we're *proud*. Jist where you fixin to *head* at mid*night?* Babylon an its sinners, woo*eee!*, may go all night, flittin ever which way, suckin the poison cup, but down here we quit early to enjoy the sleep of the just. You'll be asleep until coo-coo-roo-coo, *don't* you know that? Whut a hurry he must be *in*, whut with all the blood spillin on the highways this week-*end*. Right, boys?"

"Right!" they cried.

Mist Edward chuckled.

"Well," he said, "Ah'm goin home to mah Ossie an have me a spot of after-Thanksgivin dinner. *An* some Tums. So are these boys is mah guess. You fellas fixin to have a mite a dinner?"

"Dinner?" cried Burbank in astonishment. "Aren't you going to continue working?"

"On an empty stomach?" asked Mist Edward. "Do Ah sound like a man who'll hump hissef for a Yank while starvin? After all you Yanks have done to me an mine? Do Ah, Left? *You're* afixin to have dinner, are you, Mr. B? Well now, don't a Yank like you go jumpin to conclusions. That jist because you drive a black buck of an Emperor we don't git to eat our vittles, though they be mostly lard, chitlins, salt poke, black-eye peas, collards. We caint *all* eat high on the hog like you Northern sports."

With that Mist Edward and his crew went off to their homes, leaving Burbank to stand alone on the sidewalk, perhaps to contemplate the quality of their exhaust. He went to the highway and climbed the rise to Shorty's.

"Who owns that car graveyard east of Yazoo?" he asked Slim the barkeep over a drink.

"Mist Edward, course," Slim said with a sidelong glance.

"*Mist Edward?*" Burbank cried. "What's *he* doing owning it?"

"Heck it's oney an old junkyard," said Slim, a cord working in his neck.

"Who owns the red Emperor in it?"

"He owns that yard lock, stock and barrel."

"One hand washes the other, does it?" Burbank said. "What happened to that red Emperor?"

"Mist Edward bought it third hand, sold it to Carlow, Carlow skidded an got hissef killed."

After a while Burbank returned to the garage. The condition of Mist Edward and his colleagues was frightening. They were peering in the dimness, losing or misplacing things, plugs, hoses, bolts, washers. There finally came the moment when it was time to start the engine. Mist Edward himself turned the gold key. The engine turned over but didn't catch hold. Adjustments were made under the black hood. The engine coughed, choked. The men tinkered.

At last the engine ran. In the pre-Yazoo days it had run silently.

"What's *that?*" Burbank asked, startled. "That bagpipe playing!"

Mist Edward said casually, "Oh *that*. Exhaust leaks."

The exhaust leaks were repaired. Their place was taken by a clanking.

"What's *that?*" Burbank cried.

"The silencers," Mist Edward said. "*They'll* settle down. They're *nothin*."

"Nothing or something, they *clank*," said Burbank feverishly.

"Fuel leaks!" Spineless George shouted.

Everybody crawled under the car, searched under the hood, darted around looking for lost tools. *Fuel* leaks? Poor Burbank, to have fuel leaks at his age! And oil leaks too, it soon developed. What a dropping and misplacing of things! What a hammering, clanking!

The Emperor was finally ready to *go!* But when, after paying Mist Edward and tipping all, Burbank drove off, the gas pedal went down too far too quickly, and his gears shifted too soon, and he labored in third, and he *pinged*, and he had a ridiculous kickdown—when he pressed the gas pedal to the floor he experienced depression and despair—and his heater was out, and his generator was dead. So he returned to the garage, and more adjustments were made, and he drove off again. And that night he, Ethel, Nuncle and Flora took *off*. At last he was heading for the Keys.

The traffic was very light by mainland standards. In the long headlight beams he caught glimpses of leaves still clinging to naked branches, and broken cornstalks. The concrete highway gave way to a rough two-lane blacktop raised high above the land.

He remembered the Keys. Flying fish arrowing away from George's boat, fins whirring. The deck creaking, swaying. The line of sea showing green. Mushroom clouds rising from beyond the horizon. Milk-gray cirrus in the zenith. The bluish water, with small swells and a crisping skin, giving him a yellowtail, a couple of silver snappers, a red grouper, and then a huge barracuda (streamlined, muscular, built for speed and killing), with a cavernous mouth, protruding lower jaw, sunwashed teeth, round large staring eye. And old George handling the boat in good bare feet, bare legs strong, bare chest heaving under the jeweled Tiffany cross. (A gold ring in one ear, which he wore only in the Keys. Eccentric, but he had the dough for it.) The crewboy's left eye drooping, suggesting a deranged, criminal look.

He remembered a dream he had had last night. He was due to take part in a moon shot but he had been delayed in boarding the rocket. His face wore pancake makeup. He had to change from business clothes into his astronaut's suit. Ethel lay under her bedcovers, ignoring him in her sleepiness. As he slipped off his shirt he shouted, "I may as well move out altogether!"

He remembered Rome, going to St. Peter's, flying in the afternoon down the Italian coast, which looked brown and musty and had pockets of mist among the hills. She had kept saying how important it was for them to visit the Holy Land *soon*. Had she been afraid she'd die before seeing it, or had she hoped the Guy Upstairs would heal her broken heart? Beyond the pearly gates, in his opinion, were no angels playing Wurlitzer harps. There were only huge black holes monitored by a vast malevolent grin.

And he remembered another dream. Standing in a corner at a cocktail party, he was explaining economic theory, the balance of payments, the movement of gold out of the country. But he spoke too forcefully, in a guttural harsh voice. The group listened respectfully, fearfully, with glassy eyes, not daring to interrupt him. Then he started lecturing one guy in particular, dressed in a tweed hunting jacket almost as bulky as overcoating. Once in a while, to show who was boss, Burbank would cut out a chunk of the jacket with a sharp pocketknife. *That* shut the guy up! *That* put him in his place! But my God the guy turned out to be Jeb, his son, his own flesh and blood!

Ahead was a trailer truck, and a long curve to the right. The road was obscured by trees but Burbank moved out. He had expected to pass the truck quickly. Instead, he was inching along beside it. A car appeared, approaching him at what felt like high speed. Burbank had time to fall back. Instead, he pumped the gas pedal. The truck went stolidly forward. Burbank had no intention of giving way. He was a military man condemned by fate to a civilian life.

"Papa!" Ethel shouted.

He jammed the pedal to the floor for the kickdown, but the kickdown, like so many things before it, let him down. He aimed at the approaching car. Ethel screamed. The driver panicked and swerved off the road, which was ten or twelve feet above the land. The car went down the embankment, rolled over several times, burst into flames. Burbank passed the truck and began to leave it behind.

"My God, my God!" Ethel cried, covering her face with her freckled hands.

Burbank drove grimly on. The Keys were waiting for him, and the great marlin he was going to catch. The truck didn't slow down. It went on calmly, as if the driver had seen and heard nothing. Burbank left it increasingly behind. He took a long curve and lost sight of it. Several minutes later Ethel had a heart attack, slumped forward and seemed to pause there. She died so quietly and suddenly that Burbank, preoccupied with his thoughts, didn't realize it for some time.

FOR THE BEST IN PAPERBACKS, LOOK FOR THE

In every corner of the world, on every subject under the sun, Penguin represents quality and variety—the very best in publishing today.

For complete information about books available from Penguin—including Pelicans, Puffins, Peregrines, and Penguin Classics—and how to order them, write to us at the appropriate address below. Please note that for copyright reasons the selection of books varies from country to country.

In the United Kingdom: For a complete list of books available from Penguin in the U.K., please write to *Dept E.P., Penguin Books Ltd, Harmondsworth, Middlesex, UB7 0DA.*

In the United States: For a complete list of books available from Penguin in the U.S., please write to *Dept BA, Penguin, Box 120, Bergenfield, New Jersey 07621-0120.*

In Canada: For a complete list of books available from Penguin in Canada, please write to *Penguin Books Ltd, 2801 John Street, Markham, Ontario L3R 1B4.*

In Australia: For a complete list of books available from Penguin in Australia, please write to the *Marketing Department, Penguin Books Ltd, P.O. Box 257, Ringwood, Victoria 3134.*

In New Zealand: For a complete list of books available from Penguin in New Zealand, please write to the *Marketing Department, Penguin Books (NZ) Ltd, Private Bag, Takapuna, Auckland 9.*

In India: For a complete list of books available from Penguin, please write to *Penguin Overseas Ltd, 706 Eros Apartments, 56 Nehru Place, New Delhi, 110019.*

In Holland: For a complete list of books available from Penguin in Holland, please write to *Penguin Books Nederland B.V., Postbus 195, NL-1380AD Weesp, Netherlands.*

In Germany: For a complete list of books available from Penguin, please write to *Penguin Books Ltd, Friedrichstrasse 10-12, D-6000 Frankfurt Main I, Federal Republic of Germany.*

In Spain: For a complete list of books available from Penguin in Spain, please write to *Longman, Penguin España, Calle San Nicolas 15, E-28013 Madrid, Spain.*

In Japan: For a complete list of books available from Penguin in Japan, please write to *Longman Penguin Japan Co Ltd, Yamaguchi Building, 2-12-9 Kanda Jimbocho, Chiyoda-Ku, Tokyo 101, Japan.*

FOR THE BEST IN CONTEMPORARY AMERICAN FICTION

☐ **WHITE NOISE**
Don DeLillo

The New Republic calls *White Noise* "a stunning performance from one of our most intelligent novelists." This masterpiece of the television age is the story of Jack Gladney, a professor of Hitler Studies in Middle America, whose life is suddenly disrupted by a lethal black chemical cloud.

326 pages   ISBN: 0-14-007702-2 $6.95

☐ **IRONWEED**
William Kennedy

William Kennedy's Pulitzer Prize-winning novel is the story of Francis Phelan — ex-ball-player, part-time gravedigger, and full-time drunk.

228 pages   ISBN: 0-14-007020-6 $6.95

☐ **LESS THAN ZERO**
Bret Easton Ellis

This phenomenal best-seller depicts in compelling detail a generation of rich, spoiled L.A. kids on a desperate search for the ultimate sensation.

208 pages   ISBN: 0-14-008894-6 $6.95

☐ **THE LAST PICTURE SHOW**
Larry McMurtry

In a small town in Texas during the early 1950s, two boys act out a poignant drama of adolescence — the restless boredom, the bouts of beer-drinking, and the erotic fantasies.   *220 pages*   ISBN: 0-14-005183-X   **$5.95**

You can find all these books at your local bookstore, or use this handy coupon for ordering:

Penguin Books By Mail
Dept. BA Box 999
Bergenfield, NJ 07621-0999

Please send me the above title(s). I am enclosing _____
(please add sales tax if appropriate and $1.50 to cover postage and handling). Send check or money order—no CODs. Please allow four weeks for shipping. We cannot ship to post office boxes or addresses outside the USA. *Prices subject to change without notice.*

Ms./Mrs./Mr. _____

Address _____

City/State _____ Zip _____

Sales tax: CA: 6.5%   NY: 8.25%   NJ: 6%   PA: 6%   TN: 5.5%

FOR THE BEST IN CONTEMPORARY AMERICAN FICTION

☐ **THE WOMEN OF BREWSTER PLACE**
A Novel in Seven Stories
Gloria Naylor

Winner of the American Book Award, this is the story of seven survivors of an urban housing project — a blind alley feeding into a dead end. From a variety of backgrounds, they experience, fight against, and sometimes transcend the fate of black women in America today.

192 pages   *ISBN: 0-14-006690-X*   **$5.95**

☐ **STONES FOR IBARRA**
Harriet Doerr

An American couple comes to the small Mexican village of Ibarra to reopen a copper mine, learning much about life and death from the deeply faithful villagers. *214 pages*   *ISBN: 0-14-007562-3*   **$5.95**

☐ **WORLD'S END**
T. Coraghessan Boyle

"Boyle has emerged as one of the most inventive and verbally exuberant writers of his generation," writes *The New York Times*. Here he tells the story of Walter Van Brunt, who collides with early American history while searching for his lost father. *456 pages*   *ISBN: 0-14-009760-0*   **$8.95**

☐ **THE WHISPER OF THE RIVER**
Ferrol Sams

The story of Porter Osborn, Jr., who, in 1938, leaves his rural Georgia home to face the world at Willingham University, *The Whisper of the River* is peppered with memorable characters and resonates with the details of place and time. Ferrol Sams's writing is regional fiction at its best.

528 pages   *ISBN: 0-14-008387-1*   **$6.95**

☐ **ENGLISH CREEK**
Ivan Doig

Drawing on the same heritage he celebrated in *This House of Sky,* Ivan Doig creates a rich and varied tapestry of northern Montana and of our country in the late 1930s. *338 pages*   *ISBN: 0-14-008442-8*   **$6.95**

☐ **THE YEAR OF SILENCE**
Madison Smartt Bell

A penetrating look at the varied reactions to a young woman's suicide exactly one year later, *The Year of Silence* "captures vividly and poignantly the chancy dance of life." (*The New York Times Book Review*)

208 pages   *ISBN: 0-14-011533-1*   **$6.95**

FOR THE BEST IN CONTEMPORARY AMERICAN FICTION

☐ **IN THE COUNTRY OF LAST THINGS**
Paul Auster

Death, joggers, leapers, and Object Hunters are just some of the realities of future city life in this spare, powerful, visionary novel about one woman's struggle to live and love in a frightening post-apocalyptic world.

                   208 pages   *ISBN: 0-14-009705-8*   **$5.95**

☐ **BETWEEN C&D**
    New Writing from the Lower East Side Fiction Magazine
    Joel Rose and Catherine Texier, Editors

A startling collection of stories by Tama Janowitz, Gary Indiana, Kathy Acker, Barry Yourgrau, and others, *Between C&D* is devoted to short fiction that ignores preconceptions — fiction not found in conventional literary magazines.

                   194 pages   *ISBN: 0-14-010570-0*   **$7.95**

☐ **LEAVING CHEYENNE**
Larry McMurtry

The story of a love triangle unlike any other, *Leaving Cheyenne* follows the three protagonists — Gideon, Johnny, and Molly — over a span of forty years, until all have finally "left Cheyenne."

                   254 pages   *ISBN: 0-14-005221-6*   **$6.95**

You can find all these books at your local bookstore, or use this handy coupon for ordering:

         Penguin Books By Mail
           Dept. BA Box 999
        Bergenfield, NJ 07621-0999

Please send me the above title(s). I am enclosing _____
(please add sales tax if appropriate and $1.50 to cover postage and handling). Send check or money order—no CODs. Please allow four weeks for shipping. We cannot ship to post office boxes or addresses outside the USA. *Prices subject to change without notice.*

Ms./Mrs./Mr. _____

Address _____

City/State _____ Zip _____

Sales tax: CA: 6.5% NY: 8.25% NJ: 6% PA: 6% TN: 5.5%